To Kayla,
Enjoy reading my novel!

OLYMPIC BOUND

BY KD LEE WRITES

KD Lee Writes

Olympic Bound

Written by

KD Lee Writes

KD Lee Writes

Published by Blooming Ink Publishing, LLC

4712 East State Road 46
Bloomington, IN 47401

Copyright ©2016 by Blooming Ink Publishing, LLC
Cover art Copyright © 2016 by Blooming Ink Publishing, LLC

All rights reserved under Title 17, U.S. Code, International and Pan-American Copyright Conventions. No part of this work may be reproduced or transmitted in any form or by any means, electronic or mechanical, including but not limited to photocopying, scanning, recording, broadcast or live performance, or duplication by any information storage or retrieval system without prior written permission from the publisher, except for the inclusion of brief quotations with attribution in a review or report. To request permissions, please visit the author's website: **www.kdlwrites.com**

This book is a realistic fiction. The characters and events portrayed in this book are fictional. Any similarity to real persons (living or dead) is coincidental and not intended by the author. The author and publisher accept no responsibility of any kind for conclusions reached by readers of this book. If you do not agree with these terms, do not read this book. There is no warranty.

FIRST EDITION

ISBN: **978-1-943753-06-2**

Library of Congress Number: **2016937142**

Olympic Bound

I dedicate this book to my Grandma DD, who always encourages me to follow my dreams and who practically crawled up out of the ocean herself.

KD Lee Writes

Acknowledgements

There are many people that I would like to thank. First thank you to my mom for being my publisher and for not resting until this book was the best it could be.

Next, I want to thank my grandma for the many hours she put into editing my novels and everything else.

I can't forget to mention my little brother: he has been my biggest inspiration for many characters. I wouldn't have written *Morgan's Summer* and *Morgan's New School* without him.

Other major supports who have always believed in me are my dad and my grandpa. Thank you guys for driving me to my book signings and my golf events. You're awesome!

Thanks to Josh Gonzalez from Earwig Designs for designing a great cover. Thanks to my editors Rian Dawson and (once again) Grandma.

Last but not least (I hope I didn't forget anyone) are my readers. Without you, I wouldn't be able to be an author!

KD Lee Writes

OTHER BOOKS BY KR LEE WRITES

Morgan's Summer

A children's book full of mischief and fun, don't miss out! Ages: 8-12

Morgan's New School

This sequel to Morgan's Summer has double the trouble! Ages: 8-12

A positive thinker sees the invisible, feels the intangible and achieves the impossible.

—*Anonymous*

Olympic Bound

NOTE FROM AUTHOR

I wrote three novels before this one, and this novel was by far the most challenging. In my other novels, I knew all the information I needed beforehand; I didn't have to do any research. But for this one, I had a lot of researching to do, from searches online to checking out books at the library.

Don't get me wrong—I enjoyed writing this book—but I didn't realize how hard it would be to find out how to sign up for Qualifications for the USA Swimming Olympic Trials and everything that follows.

For research, first I turned to the Internet, every twenty-first century teenager's go-to for information. It took a long time to find anything useful that I didn't already know, and I still didn't get all my questions answered.

Next I tried the library, which, by the way, is my favorite place in the world. I asked the librarian where I could find a book on how to get into the Olympics.

I swear I stood there for about ten minutes while she searched. Not much was coming up.

Finally, she admitted it didn't look like they had much on the subject, except for a biography on a boy that went to the Olympics. She asked another librarian

KD Lee Writes

about it and he gave me something that would help: a phone number for the USA Swimming Headquarters.

I thanked the librarians, checked out the biography, and wished I could call the USA Swimming Headquarters right then, but I had a guitar lesson and a voice lesson that day.

After that, it was the weekend, and the headquarters was closed. It was painful to wait until I was finally able to call them.

When I was finally able to call them, I was very impressed with how helpful they were. They answered my phone call on the first ring. When I informed them about why I was calling, I was connected with someone who could answer my questions—all twenty of them. I was on the phone for fifteen minutes in total.

I was so excited that I could finish my book, now that I had enough reliable information to make the book as realistic and as accurate as possible.

Enjoy reading my novel!

PROLOGUE

I love swimming. I learned how to swim at the age of four in my grandma's in-ground pool. I haven't swum since my father died, though. He drowned in the ocean on our last annual summer-break vacation with my aunt in Florida. He was caught in a riptide. My mom hasn't let me get in any kind of water since then, with an exception for baths and showers (of course). It's only been a few months, but the itch to swim still hasn't left me.

From that day on, no water parks, no pool, and no fun. I'm the worst person that it could have possibly happened to. My dream since four has been to go to the Olympics. I would to sit with my dad and watch the Olympic swimmers on our TV speed through the water like jets. Dad would hug me and say, "One day that will be you, Sweet Pea."

Ever since Dad died, my mom, who is a recovering alcoholic, has struggled with staying on the wagon.

When she isn't home for dinner, I know she has been out drinking. I can smell the whiskey on her breath. She gets angry when she is drunk. Some people get silly, or depressed, but not her. She gets irritable, is inconsolable, and then goes into her room, slamming the door, to sulk in the dark. I don't see why she would want to do that to herself. I promised myself that I wouldn't ever touch a drop of alcohol.

I just don't see the point. What can you gain from that besides a nasty hangover in the morning? Sometimes I would overhear kids in the hallway at school talking about getting drunk on the weekend; I found it crazy how popular such a destructive pastime is.

I don't have much of a social life either. My routine is: get up, have a shower, make breakfast, drive my younger sister, Mel, to school, go to my school, pick up Mel, make dinner, do homework, read, watch a movie, and go to bed.

On weekends, I sometimes hang-out with my only friend, Carrie. She is nothing like me, other than we are both nerds. She hates swimming, but likes sports and dancing. She is also crazy about animals.

TABLE OF CONTENTS

ACKNOWLEDGEMENTS 7

NOTE FROM AUTHOR 11

PROLOGUE 13

CHAPTER 1 - OFFER 19

CHAPTER 2 - LOSING A FRIEND 29

CHAPTER 3 - EGG NOG!!! 49

CHAPTER 4 - FLORIDA, HERE WE COME 57

CHAPTER 5 - NORTH MANGROVE HIGH 75

CHAPTER 6 - SOARING HIGH, CRASHING LOW 89

CHAPTER 7 - THE LONGEST NIGHT 101

CHAPTER 8 - A WHOLE NEW LEVEL OF TORTURE 111

CHAPTER 9 - RELIEF 123

CHAPTER 10 - UNBELIEVABLE 141

CHAPTER 11 - PICKING UP 149

CHAPTER 12 - ONE MEDAL DOWN 159

CHAPTER 13 - STATIC	163
CHAPTER 14 – BIRTHDAY PLANNER	177
CHAPTER 15 – RANCE IT	193
CHAPTER 16 – SPARE THE TOES	199
CHAPTER 17 - PROM	205
CHAPTER 18 – LABYRINTH OF LIGHT	215
CHAPTER 19 - ANTICIPATION	223
CHAPTER 20 - QUALIFICATIONS	233
CHAPTER 21 – GOOD LUCK	245
CHAPTER 22 – BAD LUCK	255
CHAPTER 23 – NEW DISTRACTIONS	261
CHAPTER 24 - MURDERER	269
CHAPTER 25 - UNBELIEVABLE	275
CHAPTER 26 - SURPRISE	285
CHAPTER 27 – TWO SECONDS	291
CHAPTER 28 – PAY OFF	299
CHAPTER 29 – THE INTERVIEW	303
EPILOGUE	307
INTERVIEW WITH AUTHOR	311

Sophomore Year

KD Lee Writes

Olympic Bound

CHAPTER 1 – THE OFFER

I stopped in front of Mel's school and parked waiting for her to come out. When she came out, I waved out the window until she waved back, letting me know that she spotted me. She walked over and hopped in the front seat, which I strongly disapproved of.

Mel knew that I didn't want her riding in the front seat! One, it was illegal, since she wasn't old or tall enough yet, and two, she could get hurt. I looked over at her and gave her a stern look.

"I told you, you can't sit in the front, you just got out of a car seat. What if I wrecked?! Your neck would break as soon as the air bag deployed," I reprimanded.

To show how stubborn she was, Mel turned off the passenger airbag.

"Please! I am old enough, so legal now," she whined. Which wasn't really true, Mel was only just eight, and not near big enough. "Plus, you are a good driver and look the air bag is off. I won't get a broken neck now!"

"Now you will go through the window instead, and besides, even though you are old enough, you are still not big enough," I retorted. "If we didn't wreck I could get a ticket for letting you sit in the front. Get in the back."

She stuck out her tongue, got out and slammed the door. After I didn't hear the buckle click I asked, "Are you all buckled in?"

"Uhh!" she huffed.

Once she had buckled herself into the seat, I pulled out of the parking lot. She could be a little troublesome at times, but I loved her more than anyone. When I pulled into the two-car garage, I noticed Mom's car was there. She normally wouldn't be home for another half-hour or so.

"Mom is home," Mel announced, stating the obvious, like normal.

Why did she have to be so annoying?

"I noticed," I retorted, rolling my eyes.

I wondered if something had happened. Thoughts whizzed through my brain. *Did it have something to do with her drinking problem?* No, normally she would have been home past midnight, not early. *Maybe Aunt Libby invited us to stay with her in Florida? Maybe Mom is sick? Something must have happened!*

I burst through the door, out of curiosity, and saw Mom sitting with her laptop at the dining table.

"You're home!" she shouted. She swiveled around in her desk chair to face us. "There is this awesome place for sale in Florida! We can afford it if we sell this place! I am going to give an offer!"

Mom was definitely spontaneous. She had been ever since I was little, but this was a little extreme. I didn't think she was even considering moving a week ago.

"We are moving to Florida!" Mel chirped, hopping up and down.

"Yes, as long as they accept our offer," Mom said, smiling at Mel's excitement. I took a deep breath.

"What? How can we? How much is it?" I shot questions to her skeptically.

I knew we had been tight for money ever since Dad died, and Mom was known for spending money we didn't have. I almost choked when I saw the receipt for the case of wine she just *had* to have.

But she was really enthusiastic, I could tell, so I tried to make it sound like I was just curious instead of criticizing her. I had never seen her be this eager before, so I knew it meant a lot to her. *No one is happy when she gets in a bad mood.*

"Oh, Taylor, you and your numbers," Mom said. "I don't want you worrying like you did when we spent all that money on the trip to Scotland."

I cringed. I had every reason to worry. We couldn't pay our next month's credit card bill or the one after. Credit cards have a crazy amount of interest, which didn't help our situation any. Luckily, she finally sold the house she was counting on selling to pay everything off.

"I was just curious," I replied, shrugging. "That is all." I tried to keep things light, while attempting to weasel the information out of her.

"Is it close to the beach?!" Mel questioned, still bouncing on her toes. Mom shed a tear and her happy face turned to a gloomy one.

"You know I don't want you to go to the beach, Mel; that's how your father died," she said.

My dad was the one that always encouraged me to swim. Our hope was that one day I would make it to the Olympics, but that dream was flushed down the drain when he was swept up in a riptide off the coast of Key West in Florida during the summer.

Mom went ballistic when it happened. First, she went on a major drinking binge and even missed the funeral! Then she banned me from all pools and other large bodies of water.

Olympic Bound

I almost went crazy at that point. Not only did I lose my dad, but I lost my swimming privileges, too! Swimming was my life. Somehow I managed to keep it together. I had to for Mel's sake.

Poor Mel lost both parents that day: Dad was dead and Mom was catatonic with grief. Someone needed to take charge. Mel needed me and so did Mom. They both still relied on me for many things.

With Mom's philosophy of spending money like you have to spend it all while you're still alive, I'd have to get a job soon, before she used up all the money we got from the insurance agency after Dad's death.

"But at least can I play in the sand?" Mel asked. "I won't touch the water!"

"No! I am sorry, Mel, but I can't lose you, too," Mom said.

Another tear fell down her cheek. She wiped her face with the back of her hand.

I hoped Mel wouldn't drag the argument out any longer, causing Mom another breakdown. It had been months since Dad had passed, but none of us were even close to over it.

Mel seemed to handle it better than any of us, but she was young and was not as close to him as I was. With his death, I wasn't allowed to swim anymore, which freed up all of my time to be with her. Her love of me and getting more time with me buffered the loss of Dad. But, Mel hated that she couldn't swim either.

"It isn't fair!" Mel said. Mom blinked back more tears.

"Stop! End of discussion!" Mom cried, breathing deep breaths, trying to calm herself. We didn't say another word. Then she started speaking again, as if she had forgotten all about the argument. "Come look at this place you two! Here are some pictures," she said, bringing images of the house up on her computer screen.

The house was cute with a great view of a canal. There was a kitchen, two bedrooms, and a living room/dining room/TV room. There were two bathrooms, one of which was in the master bedroom right next to the walk-in closet. It did look small though, maybe only a thousand square feet, way smaller than our house. It would be a major down-size for us.

"Mom, what about your job?" I asked. Real estate was the one thing she was good at, and it was the perfect job for her since she loved to look at houses.

"My job? That is easy! I called one of the real state agencies already, and I'm going to fill in an empty spot," she said. "They seemed impressed with some of the houses I have sold. They did seem a little desperate though." Mom tapped her chin thoughtfully. I looked through the pictures some more.

Olympic Bound

Moving to this tiny place did not seem very appealing to me, but Mom was stubborn, and once she thought up an idea, it was impossible to talk her out of it. If I said anything besides how I thought it was a great idea now, it would just turn into an argument, and she would still be determined to buy the place anyway.

"So, will me and Taylor still have to share a room?" Mel asked.

"Yes, I am afraid so, Honey," said Mom. "But we can't afford to stay in this big house, the yard is too much for me to handle, and the memories are just much too raw."

Mel started dancing around the room and chanting as if she didn't even care. Maybe she didn't. I did though, and having Mel as a roommate was not the best thing in the world.

"We are moving to Florida! We are moving to Florida! We are moving to Florida! We are moving to Florida! Does that mean I won't see my friends anymore?" Mel asked, eventually.

"No, I guess not," Mom sighed. "You will make new friends, though, I'm sure."

"That's ok, I guess. I'll miss my friends, but at least Mean Maggie won't be there," she said. She started chanting again. Mom placed the offer and I called Carrie.

"We might be moving to Florida," I told her as soon as she picked up.

"What? Florida! That is like a billion miles away!" Carrie shrieked, dramatically. She was the most dramatic person I had ever met. "You are my favorite friend! You can't do this to me!"

"Carrie, calm down," I said. "Nothing is certain, but you know how my mom is when she gets an idea stuck in her head." I didn't really want to move to Florida even though Aunt Libby lived down there. It was too rainy in the summer and way too hot!

"We can call each other. I'll call every day!" Carrie promised, as if she was already certain I was leaving.

I sighed. "Like I said, it's just a maybe," I replied. "We may not be moving."

"Sure, sure," Carrie puffed, sarcastically. "Well, I have to go."

"Ok, I have to start dinner anyway. See you, Carrie."

"Alright, bye, Taylor!"

I hung up and stuffed my phone into my pocket. I grabbed a carton of three-cheese tortellini out of the fridge and filled a pot half way with water.

Cooking wasn't one of my favorite things to do, but I was the only one willing to do it. So, I filled a pot half-full with water, put the pot on the stove, and twisted the dial to high. The flames caught underneath. I waited until the water boiled to put in the pasta. I chopped up vegetables, mixed them with spinach and lettuce for a salad.

***

"Dinner is ready!" I called, after I had dished out the pasta into bowls and set the table. I put the salad in the middle, so Mom and Mel could serve themselves.

Mel twirled her food around with her fork and didn't bother to get any salad. "You ok?" I asked.

"Yes! I am so excited, I can't eat," she said, sarcastically, rolling her eyes.

Mom used sarcasm a lot, but so did I. Mel could have picked it up from either of us. I thought back, trying to figure out what she might have to be upset about. It wasn't the move—Mel was excited for that. But I couldn't think of anything else.

"What is wrong then?" I asked.

"Nothing," she answered.

"Mel, stop that. Something is wrong, obviously," Mom said, through a mouth-full of salad.

"I just remembered that if we move to Florida, I can't do my play," Mel pointed out, sadly.

I scanned my brain. Mel never said anything about a play before...

"What play?" I asked.

"It was going to be a surprise. It is the day before Christmas break, and I have the leading role," she answered.

"That is only a week away," I replied. "We won't have moved by then."

"We won't? Yes!" Mel cried.

Suddenly, her appetite returned, and she dug into her plate of food.

"So what's this play about?" I asked, looking down at her.

"It is called 'A Bit of Applause for Mrs. Claus.' It is about how Santa Claus always gets the credit and Mrs. Claus and the elves do most of the work," Mel replied.

"Sounds cute, good for you for doing it," I said, patting her on the back.

We finished dinner and went to bed.

I told you, I lead a plain life.

Chapter 2 - Losing a Friend

The week flew by. It was the day before Christmas Break—the day of Mel's play. We gathered around the table for breakfast and afterward made our way to the school to watch Mel's performance.

Everyone Mel knew was there; our Aunt Libby, all the kids in her class, the teachers, and even Mom's grandparents, who are grouchy and hate to leave their house. Dad's sister, Gemma, and a few others joined us, too.

Mel would be great, I was sure. She was fearless, smart and a little ostentatious. Santa Claus was the first on stage—he was played by a plump little boy.

"My sweet Mrs. Claus will you get the reindeer groomed while I test your homemade cookies?" he asked.

Mel came on stage.

"Yes, Honey," said Mel speaking as Mrs. Claus. She began singing a song about the reindeer while she groomed them. Then, she cleaned the workshop and helped the elves make the toys.

I should mention that the whole play was written by her third grade class—that was very obvious. Mel started singing another song.

"Work and work, that is all I ever do," she sang. *"Cook, and clean and sweep, it's true."*

The elves began singing after her, *"Santa Claus sits and tastes, he eats it all and never wastes."* While the elves sang, Santa Claus just sat and munched his cookies.

"May I come with you, jolly old soul, because I really want to go," Mel continued singing. She kept singing until just before Santa left for his Christmas Eve rounds.

"It's time for me to go, but let's not get in a row," Mr. Claus sang. *"You can't come with me. You're too old you see."*

They had a singing battle and Mr. Claus won. He left and Mel finished off with one more song.

I sat through it for Mel's sake, but the show was easily the worst play I'd ever been to, by far! At least Mel's singing voice was easy to listen to. She was one of the few that could actually sing. It is kind of ironic too, since her name is Melody.

"He works once a season," she sang. "We work 300 times that for no particular reason. He should just use his magic, but he says he doesn't have on him his magical gadget." She continued singing until everyone came back out on stage and took their bows.

I clapped my hands until they hurt, just because Mel deserved the attention. Then I put my fingers to my mouth and whistled as loudly as I could. Her acting and singing did help the show despite the horrible lines the kids came up with.

When Mel came off stage, Mom and I wrapped her up in a hug.

"Good Job! You were great!" I said.

Mom agreed.

"How long did you practice before the play?" I asked wondering how long she had kept this secret from us.

"Two and a half weeks of school," she said. "They had me take home copies of the songs so I would have more time to learn them."

"Well, I am proud of you, Sweetheart," Mom said.

***

We went home, and I grabbed a banana for lunch to take up to my room. Only moments later, Mom knocked on my door. I was simply reading, so I told her to come in.

She opened the door and cried out, "They accepted the offer, and I found a bank willing to give me the loan! The closing will be three weeks after Christmas, on the fifteenth of January!" Her smile extended almost up to her ears.

"Really! Awesome! What school will I go to?" I asked with false excitement. Mom didn't seem to notice or pretended not to at least.

"I looked at a couple schools, and I found out that in Florida, you don't go to school based on the school district you live in," Mom said. "Instead, they let you chose your favorite three, and they try to place you with your first pick. If there isn't a spot for you, they will try to put you in your second pick, and it keeps going like that. I'll look for schools with good ratings."

"I'll look into it, too," I said. "What is the address of the house?"

"I will find that out," Mom offered. "Oh, and it's a condo, not a house. I thought I showed you the street view picture."

"Oh, no," I said. "I don't think you did."

"Sorry, ok. I'll go get the address," she chortled. "Be back in a blink." She closed the door as she left.

So they accepted the offer, I thought to myself, *I'm probably moving to Florida.*

Mel ran into our room and cried out, snapping me out of my reverie.

"Did you hear? They accepted the offer! We are moving to Florida!" she squealed with delight.

"Something still could go wrong," I said cautiously. "Like the bank deciding not to give us the loan." I was secretly hopeful that the loan wouldn't come through, and we could stay put.

"No," Mel assured. "Mom said that she got a bank that will give us the loan."

"They could still change their minds," I said.

"That sucks!" she exclaimed. "I hope we get to move to Florida."

"We'll see," I told her.

Maybe Florida wouldn't be so bad. I could go sunbathing on the beach. I wouldn't tell Mom. I could go swimming in the ocean. Again, I wouldn't tell Mom.

Mel left my room just as Mom came back with the address. I put it into the search engine and looked up a few things online. Then Mel rejoined us.

"Taylor, will you play tea party with me?" she asked. She began to set up her little foldout Cinderella table with teacups, putting her stuffed animals into the chairs gathered around it.

"Yeah, I guess I don't have anything better to do," I said.

My phone let out a shrill ring. I reached into my pocket, fished it out, and answered the call.

"Hello?" I said.

"Hi, it's Carrie, I'm coming over," she said, but her voice had a strained edge to it.

"Wha-" I tried to ask a question, but Carrie cut me off before I could finish.

"No time to explain. Bye!" She hung up. I stuffed the phone back into my pocket.

"Who was that?" asked Mel.

"Carrie," I said. "She's coming over,"

Mel scrunched her eyebrows and stuck out her lower lip, putting on her best pouty face.

"I'll play the game until she gets here," I frowned.

"But she only lives five minutes away!" Mel pouted. She folded her arms across her chest.

"Well, we better start playing then, before it is too late," I advised. We clinked our teacups together, holding our pinkies out until the doorbell rang.

"I'll get it!" I yelled and set down my teacup before racing for the door. I tossed the door open, and Carrie was on the other side weeping. She wasn't bawling, but tears were dripping down her cheeks, and her eyes were red and puffy.

"My parents were fighting again, but this time it was really bad," Carrie intoned. "I had to get away from them, and you are moving so I wanted to hang out."

"So you would have gone to another friend's house, if I wasn't leaving?" I asked, teasingly.

"You know what I mean," she said.

"I know," I said. "I'm just kidding."

"Are you going to let me in, or are you going to let me stand out here and freeze to death?" She asked.

"Yes, come on in," I laughed and stepped out of the way to let her in. She knocked the snow off her shoes and came inside. Taking off her shoes, she followed me into my room.

Mel was there; I asked if she would leave. You can guess her answer. Not wanting to talk in front of Mel, I asked Mom if Carrie and I could talk in her room. Mom said yes, so Carrie and I sat on her bed and talked.

"Any day now," sniff, "Any day now, they are going to, sep-a-rate." She spoke that last word with difficulty through her tears.

"I'm sorry, Carrie," I sighed. "I know how you feel."

"No, you don't," Carrie wailed. "Your parents didn't separate!"

"No," I snapped. "Something worse happened. My dad died! At least you still will get to see both your parents! I would trade almost anything to be in your shoes instead of mine."

"Oh! I am so sorry, Taylor, I forgot…"

"I know," I immediately felt sorry for getting angry at her. Changing the subject, I asked, "How long are you staying?"

"'Until three-fifty," Carrie answered. "Or as long as it is ok with your mom. My mom just said to be back for dinner."

"Yeah, Mom won't care," I agreed.

"What are we going to do now?" Carrie asked.

"We could paint our nails," I said, as I stood up.

"Sure," Carrie agreed. We went into my room. I grabbed the nail polish remover and my collection of nail polish and nail stickers.

"Can I paint my nails, too?!" Mel asked when she saw the supplies I was gathering.

"Sure," I said.

"You are too good of a sister," Carrie said.

"I want pink!" Mel yelled. "Pink! Pink! Pink!"

"Here," I said passing to her the bottle of bright pink polish. She started on her nails immediately. Meanwhile, I started working on Carrie's toenails. I removed the bright yellow nail polish that was left over from the last time we'd done this. Then, I started applying a glittery blue nail polish. On her fingernails, I put on a pink polish followed by flower-nail stickers after the polish dried.

I'm not sure what kind of flowers they were—maybe daisies? It was hard to tell, but they were still pretty.

Then, Carrie started painting my nails, but with the opposite color scheme: pink and flower-nail stickers on my toenails and glittery blue on my fingernails.

"There, done," she said, as she tried to return the nail polish. It tipped over and glittery blue goop oozed out on the hardwood. Carrie cussed and then immediately covered her mouth.

"Sorry, Mel! I didn't mean to say that in front of you."

"Here, I got it," I said, blowing on my nails.

"No, here, I'll get it," she said.

I tipped the nail polish back up the right way and Carrie went to get something to clean up the mess. She returned with a wet rag.

"Sorry about that," she apologized while she cleaned up the mess. It came up easily since it was still wet. "What are we going to do now?" She asked.

"We could watch something on Netflix," I suggested.

"Sure, Netflix is great," Carrie responded. We sat on the couch and it wheezed under our weight. We looked under genre and picked the romance section. We picked a romantic comedy called *You've Got Mail*. It was romantic, funny, and cleverly written.

"When are you going to play Tea Party with me?!" Mel demanded, angrily when the movie was over.

"Fine, I will do it for a bit, right now," I answered.

"Yay!" she said and ran to our room.

"You want to play with us?" I asked Carrie.

Olympic Bound

"No, definitely not," Carrie replied. "I think you are the only girl at school who would do that with her sister while a friend is over!"

"Shut up," I said, and she followed me to my room. All three of us (yes, including Carrie) sat down at Mel's mini table.

"I feel so idiotic!" Carrie complained, as she picked up a teacup. She looked surprised to actually see tea in the teacup.

"Would you prefer coffee my good man?" Mel questioned Carrie.

"I am a girl," Carrie grumbled.

"I know; I just like saying it," Mel giggled.

"Yes, I would prefer coffee," Carrie finally joined in the fun, but still wore a grim expression. Mel poured her some coffee.

"Would you like cream or sugar?" Mel questioned.

"Yes, both," Carrie replied, feeling ridiculous.

"How many cubes?" Mel asked.

"One," Carrie said. Mel added some cream and a cube of sugar.

"Here," Mel said and passed the teacup to Carrie. Carrie stirred it and complained as soon as the stuff hit her lips.

"It's cold!"

"Nuke it," I said. Carrie got up and went to the kitchen. I sipped on my room-temperature Sniffles Herbal Tea with Mel until she came back.

"After I finish the coffee, I am going to head out," Carrie said.

"What! Why?" I asked.

"Why do you think?" she replied "We're playing Tea Party with your little sister."

"Ok, I'll stop." I said. "I know it isn't your thing, but if I didn't do this for her, she would have to play by herself all the time. Mom won't play with her."

"Oh! Boo-hoo! Waa! Waa! She'll live," Carrie said, rolling her eyes. "Why don't her friends come over?"

"They do on weekends sometimes, but normally, they're busy," Mel piped up.

"You know, Taylor, you are never going to have any fun if you keep being a Mom to your sister!" Carrie nagged. "Come on, let's go have some fun!" Carrie encouraged. "Grab your purse." I went to retrieve my purse, and then I followed Carrie into the kitchen.

Olympic Bound

"Bye, Mrs. Reeve, we are going out for a bit," Carrie said.

"Make sure you're back in time to make dinner, Taylor!" Mom called after us.

"Ok!" I called back, hoping Carrie didn't have anything too crazy in mind. Mom was engrossed in a documentary, so I don't think she heard my reply. We got into Carrie's car and drove off.

I didn't ask questions because I knew I wouldn't get the answer to them. We stopped at the mall. Of course! I should have known! Carrie's car always finds its way to the mall when Carrie is behind the wheel. We walked in, and Carrie stopped in front of a makeup shop.

"Carrie, the only makeup I do is Chap Stick and nail polish," I said. "And trust me; I have enough of that stuff at home."

"Please, it will only take a second!" Carrie begged.

"Fine!" I retorted. I began counting. "One second, two seconds, three seconds."

"Ok, ten minutes then," Carrie groaned. She snatched up a few lipsticks, blush, and eye shadow. She stuffed one of the lipsticks in her purse and then paid for the others at the cash register.

"I saw that!" I whispered to her when she was done.

"Saw what?" She asked, innocently.

"You just shoplifted!" I hissed, through clenched teeth.

"I only took the burden of the clerk having to ring up seven things instead of six," she said. "They were over charging anyway."

Carrie hadn't ever shoplifted before, that I knew of. That was awful! I wondered . . . *does she do that often?* I wasn't sure I wanted to know the answer.

"That is wrong!" I told her. "You can't do stuff like that! That store is someone's living!"

"It's their fault!" Carrie countered. "If they hadn't charged so much for it, I would have paid. You try it,"

"What? No!" I exclaimed.

"Try it," Carrie said, putting her arm around me.

"But . . . what if I get caught,"

"Just be sneaky with it!" Carrie whispered.

"No, no, I won't do it!" I said "That is stealing! You wouldn't steal something from my room would you?"

"No!" Carrie hissed in less of a whisper.

"See, it's not right." I replied.

"Fine," Carrie said, as she rolled her eyes.

What I really wanted to do was get on the bungee jumping trampoline. They had them set up in the mall. They strap you to bungee cords and you jump. The bungee cords make you go higher than you normally would. It may be childish, but it's actually really fun.

I asked Carrie if she was interested, but she wasn't. She was more interested in following this boy, Ryan, from school. She did it for a tiny bit until she realized he was with his girlfriend, Sandy Sparks. Carrie hated Sandy Sparks: Sandy was pretty, popular, and rude. She was extremely rude to people like us, but I couldn't blame her if that meant she was being rude to shoplifting stalkers.

"Carrie, you know I don't like shopping! Can we go home?" I begged. I had never enjoyed shopping, and I was starting to get tired of all of Carrie's shenanigans.

When I was little, my mom would go shopping for clothes for me. She started taking me along when I was ten. Then, when I was thirteen, she began to just drop me off at the mall and letting me fend for myself. Now she doesn't have anything to do with it.

"Fine, let me just grab one more thing," she said, and then stuffed a watch into her purse.

"Hey! That girl just shoplifted!" The lady at the cash register cried. She picked up her cell phone and started to dial.

"Run!" Carrie said.

"But I didn't do it!" I shrieked.

"Run!" She repeated. So I ran; I could run fast. All the bullies at school when I was younger could never catch me. So I passed Carrie, and I passed the cops. WAIT! WHAT!? THE COPS!? SHOOT! *I didn't mean that literally, don't shoot.*

They started running after me. They ignored Carrie, as she merged in with the crowd of shoppers.

The cops were fast and I was getting tired. Eventually, they caught up with me.

***

"Is this her?" The officer asked holding on to my shirt. As if I was going to try to run again!

"Yes, but I didn't actually see her steal. I saw the other girl steal," the lady, who had called the cops, said. "But they were together, so I think she stole something, too. Why else would she run?"

Great, I knew that I shouldn't have run. If I had listened to my gut, instead of Carrie, I wouldn't have been in this predicament to start with.

"Give me your purse," the cop said. I handed it over and he rummaged through it while the other cop checked my pockets.

"Did she take this?" He said holding up a nail polish.

"We might have something like that, let me check." I hadn't stolen the nail polish. I had bought it at the next store over.

"I got that at a different store," I said.

"So you stole from more than one store?" the clerk questioned.

"NO! I didn't steal from any store," I corrected. "It was just my friend, Carrie." The lady held up a nail polish just like the one I had bought at the other store.

"Ah-ha, here is a nail polish that is identical. You are a thief!" The lady said. I noticed her name tag, the clerk was named Evelin.

"I didn't steal anything!" Then I remembered I had the receipt! In my panic, I had almost forgotten! I snatched my purse back and searched through it.

"I have the receipt!" I explained.

I rummaged through my wallet and there it was. I pulled it out, read it, and passed it to the officer. He read it, too.

"I am going to let you off with a warning," the first cop said. He was still clutching onto my shirt, but then he let go.

"Where can we find Carrie?" Both cops asked me.

I paused, thinking for a moment. I was moving to Florida anyway, so Carrie couldn't make my life a living hell if I betrayed her. So I decided to help the officers. She shouldn't have shoplifted anyway. It was wrong. Plus, she betrayed me by leaving me to take the blame.

Then I got an idea. I knew that it would be disloyal to her, but Carrie had never been the perfect friend either. Shoot, she was the one that had gotten me into this whole mess! So I told the cops I would help them get Carrie. I got out my phone and dialed her number.

"I got off with a warning, where should I meet you?" I paused as I listened to her reply.

"Ok, see you there," I said.

"She is going to meet me at the pizzeria," I told the cops. "Don't let her see you."

***

"Hey! Over here!" Carrie said, waving when she spotted me. I sat down next to her. It didn't take long for the cops to make themselves known.

Long story short, since she had dumped the stuff she had stolen before leaving the store, they couldn't charge her with anything. So, like they had done to me, they let her off with a warning. They did call her parents, nonetheless.

Olympic Bound

I felt a little bad for her, too. I hated having to rat her out, but it wasn't like the police wouldn't have found her without me. I had just made their job easier.

But man, she had a hell-house to go back to. Her parents aren't the, forgive—and—forget type.

For once, I was glad to be moving to Florida.

KD Lee Writes

CHAPTER 3 – EGGNOG!!!

"Wake up! Come on! I want to open my presents!" Mel was literally jumping on my stomach. I looked over at the clock.

4:36 A.M.

"Mel, get off," I groaned. "It's too early! Go back to bed," I put my pillow over my head, and Mel tried to give me a Wet Willie.

"Mel!" I shot straight up with a start. I quickly realized this was exactly what she had hoped for. The little brat! I was wide awake now. Great, this sucked!

"Mel, don't wake me up like that ever again!" I ordered.

Not able to stay mad at her for long, I rolled out of bed and followed her to where the Christmas tree was. She looked through the presents, found one with my name on it and passed it to me.

The package was small and square. Whatever was inside was wrapped in red and green wrapping paper. I ripped it open. I didn't bother waiting for Mom to wake up. Who knows how long it would take her to rouse from her medicated sleep.

Inside were three CDs. Noel Jenkins? Mom knows I don't like her music, or at least she would if she ever paid attention to me. The next CD was Katy Perry. OK. I gave her credit for that. I actually liked Katy's music. The last one was Selina Gomez. Her music was ok, too. But WOW, what lame presents.

"Look, Taylor! A make-up kit!" Mel said.

"Yeah, cool," I said smiling at her. All my anger evaporated in that moment because she looked so excited.

"Taylor! Look! An American Doll!" Mel exclaimed.

"Hey! Are you guy's opening presents without me?" Mom shouted from the top of the stairs. She dashed down the steps, tying her robe firmly around her waist as she went.

"Yes," said Mel, ripping open another present.

Christmas was still my favorite time of year. Admittedly, it was mostly because of the all you-can-drink eggnog. Eggnog just happened to be one of my all-time favorite drinks. It was a special treat for me, because I only got it around this time of year.

Another thing I liked about Christmas was how happy it made Mel. *When she is happy, so is Mom.* We all became such a depressing bunch after Dad died. It just wasn't the same without him. He would tell jokes and guzzle more eggnog than all of us combined, which was crazy since I am such an eggnog lover.

He must have gained ten pounds each Christmas day. Not that he was a big guy, but with all that eggnog I wondered how he fit though the front door! He would make us laugh. He even dressed up as Santa for Mel one year. Dad also loved to sing. We would go out and sing like Christmas Carolers. His favorite Christmas song was "Silver Bells." He would sing that one until he went hoarse.

A tear rolled down my face as the memories flooded back, but I caught it before anyone noticed. It had seemed so long since he passed away, but it was just last summer. Still, it hasn't gotten any better. I still missed him.

Only three weeks left until we were going to be closing on our new house. Even though I refused to admit it, I was beginning to get excited about the move.

"Three weeks," I said.

"Three weeks until what?" Mel asked.

"Until the closing on our new house in Florida," I replied.

"Yay!" Mel squealed.

"Eggnog, anyone?" Mom asked us.

"YEAH!" Mel said, hopping up. She might be an eggnog addict like the rest of my family, but she couldn't match my love of eggnog.

"Sure, I will have some, too," I joined in.

"Three cups o' eggnog, coming up!" Mom said. She hurried to the kitchen and came back with three glasses filled to the brim with eggnog. We cozied up on the couch and drank greedily.

"Would you guys like some sugar cookies?" I asked.

"Yes, thank you," Mom replied.

"Yeah!" Mel shouted. She was right next to me and her shout set my ears ringing.

"Are you trying to make my ears bleed?" I asked.

"No," she said, looking down, abashed.

I baked the sugar cookies and refilled Mom and Mel's eggnog. When the cookies where ready, I asked them if they wanted to watch *Dear Santa* on Netflix. It was pretty good. The main actress wasn't very good though, and I didn't like her character either.

Olympic Bound

***

A few days after Christmas, Mom came into my room bearing bad news. It put a damper on my Christmas high. Why did she have to do something like this right after Christmas?

"Taylor, I have some bad news," Mom said, as she walked into my room. She was wrapping the bottom of her shirt around her finger. That was a weird habit she had, and has had for as long as I could remember. But the only time she did it was when something was very wrong. I took a deep breath, eyeing her nervous twitch and the worry lines over her eyebrows.

"What is it?" I asked, wanting her to get on with it.

"First, don't get mad, OK?" she asked.

"OK," I agreed cautiously.

"I had to sell your car. We needed the money," she blurted out.

I was shocked. Had I understood her? A burst of anger coursed through me. Then, I saw in her eyes that she was truly ashamed. I really felt like yelling at her. I wanted to exclaim that if money was that tight, then she shouldn't have even looked into places in Florida.

But instead of taking my anger out on her, I took a couple deep breaths to calm myself. Yelling at her wouldn't change anything.

"Say something," Mom begged.

I realized that she probably would have preferred me to yell at her. At least then she would know how to handle the situation. It probably startled her that I was just sitting there, staring perplexedly at her.

My throat was so tight, all I could do was whisper, "How could you do that? It wasn't yours to sell."

My car was my one freedom. Mom had given it to me for my sixteenth birthday. It was a gift given to me and not hers to sell.

"By law, it was," she said, and she squeezed her eyes shut, pinching the bridge of her nose. "Taylor, I am sorry, but I couldn't get a big enough loan."

"Please just get out," I said, looking away from her. I loved my car. How could she do something like that?

"Taylor, I should have said something to you, first. I just—" she started to say, but I cut her off.

"Just, please get out," I said, shaking my head in disbelief.

Mom nodded, tears glistening in her hazel eyes. She left my room without another word.

I still didn't want to accept that she had sold—SOLD—my car. But it didn't change the fact that she did.

Olympic Bound

***

By the time the closing came around, we were too excited to talk about anything else. I had finally come around to liking the idea of moving to Florida. Yet, I still hadn't forgiven Mom about my car.

"Hurry up! We are going to be late!" Mom yelled.

We scrambled into Mom's little Kia. She had let us skip school, because she felt it was important that we see how a closing was done. There wasn't really much to it: signing paperwork and meeting the new owners was about the extent of it.

***

When we returned home, we started packing our stuff for the moving truck.

"Mel, go out in the snow and play. You may never see it in person again," I told her. Out of all the things I would miss about Indiana, snow was definitely one of them. Now, snow was going to be the one thing that would seem farthest from my reach.

"No! I hate snow!" Mel complained. "It's cold and wet and you have to bundle yourself up until you can't move!"

I rolled my eyes. What eight-year-old doesn't like to play in the snow?

"Ok, then," I said. I let it drop.

The moving truck got here three days later, so we already had everything packed and ready to go. Mel had to go around the house and say bye to everything— each room, each door, and so on. She wanted me to join her, but I didn't see the point. It wasn't as if the stuff could hear. She also had to hug and kiss the walls.

"Bye, stain! Bye, bedroom! Bye, bathroom! Bye, toilet plunger! Bye, sink!" You get the point.

I will have to admit, after leaving the house and looking at it for the last time; I quietly whispered my own goodbye. I would miss this place. It contained so many memories of my dad. The moment the house was out of sight, it felt like Dad was truly dead.

Olympic Bound

Chapter 4 – Florida, Here We Come

"Are we there yet?" Mel asked.

"No, no, no for the hundredth time, no! We only left an hour ago!" Mom muttered.

"How much longer?" Mel grumbled.

"Five minutes ago I said I don't know; I still don't know!" Mom grumbled.

"Well, how long, roughly?" Mel asked, again.

"Ten days!" Mom said sarcastically. I think she probably rolled her eyes, too.

"Was that sar-case-mm?" Mel asked.

"Sarcasm," I corrected. "And yes, it was sar-case-mm, as you call it." I said. This was going to be a long road trip.

Mom loves country music. I hate it. And guess what we were constantly listening to-country.

"I am about to rip my ear drums out if you don't turn down that country music!" I cried.

Mom let out a groan. "I already turned it down all the other times you asked," she said, exasperated and annoyed.

"Then could you at least switch the station?" I pleaded.

She switched the station, angrily; I groaned. More country! I was mistaken earlier. This was going to be a really, *really*, long road trip.

Mel put on her earbuds and plugged them into her iPod. Ugh, why hadn't I thought of that? I scrambled for my own earbuds, connected them to my phone, and started listening to my favorite song. I looked over at Mel and she was playing the game Zombie Tower.

"Die!" she cried. Maybe videogames *are* causing violence...

***

As we drove, we passed a dozen cow pastures and even a windmill farm. We drove late into the night. Mel fell asleep around 10:30 P.M. The last thing I remembered was seeing the clock turn to midnight. I woke up in the morning, and we were still driving.

"Did you drive all the way though?" I asked.

"No, I stopped and rested shortly after you dozed off," Mom said, peaking at me though the rear-view mirror.

"You look tired," I said.

"Well, what do you expect? I am not Super Woman, you know," she said, with a slight smile playing at her lips.

I realized that my earbuds were still in, so I took them out; my phone had died because I left it playing music all night, so now I wouldn't have use for the earbuds anyway.

Mel was still sleeping soundly and curled up against the tinted window. I glanced at the clock. It was 9:30 A.M. When we didn't have an alarm clock beside us, Mel and I were night owls.

Then I thought about school. When will I start school again? I had picked out a few schools I liked in the area, but I still wasn't sure where I would actually be going.

I looked out the window. It was raining. Good, at least it wasn't snow. The rain was really coming down hard, though. It was difficult to see very far ahead of us.

I couldn't look at the view because the rain made visibility so bad, and I couldn't use my phone since it was dead, so I grabbed Mel's iPod. Shoot! She had it password protected. I had nothing to lose, so I started to guess what it might be.

This is Mel we are talking about; it can't be that hard to guess. 0000, nope; 1111, nope. Then I tried 1234, and it worked! I looked through the games she had, but nothing interested me. Mel just had stuff like Zombie Tower and Beauty Shop. I put back her iPod and focused on the radio. Finally, there was a non-country song so I began to sing along.

"*I gave, gave you my heart! You gave, gave it away. I saved, saved you my love. You threw, threw it away.*" It wasn't the best song, but it was ok, if not a little corny. I wished I had remembered to put the car charger up with us. But unfortunately, it was somewhere in the back of the moving van. So instead, I pulled out a notepad from the pocket on the back of the seat and looked around for a pencil or pen. I found a pen in the door slot and started drawing. I wasn't in the mood for much else.

I sketched a portrait of Mel's face with the messy hair and all. I admired my work when I was done. It wasn't Leonardo Da Vinci's Mona Lisa or anything, but it was pretty good all the same.

As I sketched more strands of hair, Mel woke up. Her eyes were barely open, as if her eyelids were struggling against the sands of sleep. She looked around and, of course, her first words were. "Are we there, yet?"

Mom replied, exasperated, "No! You will know when we are there."

Olympic Bound

As we continued to drive, the rain began to let up. Around noon, Mel complained, "I am starving!"

"Ok, start looking for signs," Mom said. "We should be able to find something."

"There's a Taco Bell up on the right if you want something quick," I said.

"McDonalds!" Mel cried.

"That would be quick, too," Mom agreed. "But Taco Bell is closer; let's go there," Mom decided.

"Are we going through the drive-thru?" I asked.

"Yes, so tell me what you girls want," Mom said, while she switched from the fast lane to the exit lane. I thought for a moment. Taco Bell's soft-shell tacos are pretty good, might as well get that.

"Could we eat inside, please?" Mel begged.

"No, we are in a hurry," Mom said.

"Why?" Mel asked.

"First, you can't wait to get there, now you don't want me to hurry! Make up your mind," Mom fumed, as we pulled into Taco Bell's parking lot.

"I want four tacos! With lettuce, cheese, and beef," Mel said. We drove around the building to the machine that takes the drive-thru orders.

"Welcome to Taco Bell, may I take your order?" The guy at the other end of the machine said. He sounded devastatingly bored. Who wouldn't be working this kind of job?

"Yes," Mom replied. "We will have four standard soft-shell tacos, three standard hard-shell tacos, one large diet cola, and two small waters."

"Wait, I wanted four hard-shell tacos!" Mel whimpered.

"Your eyes are bigger than your stomach," Mom disputed. "You can't even finish three."

Mel huffed and crossed her arms, as we pulled up to the first window. Mom paid, and we moved up to the second. After we got our food, Mel scarfed down her three tacos and said, "I'm still hungry!"

Mom simply ignored her. She just breathed deeply. After she did a bit of silent meditating, she said, "Mel, don't push my buttons. Ok? I am on the verge," Mom warned.

"The verge of what?" she asked. *Doesn't she get that is going to egg mom on?* I elbowed her, slightly, in her side.

"Ow!" she screeched, over exaggerating.

"Shh," I whispered.

Olympic Bound

Mom paid no more attention to us. She kept her eyes on the road, gripping the steering wheel so hard that her knuckles were white, and you could see the veins in the back of her hands.

Mel got her iPod out; I looked at it, longingly. I wished I had my car charger! Instead of listening to it, though, Mel decided to play with the dolls that she had brought with it. Because I didn't have anything to block out the nuisance, I had to listen to her little chats. She began talking to her grizzly bear named Damian, from Build-a-Bear.

"When we get to Florida, I will find my brush and get you all combed up," she began. "You will look so handsome. Jenny will have to like you! You can even lie out in the sun with me if you want. Mom won't let me show you the beach or the pool though. She is so strict! She just misses Daddy." Mel hugged the bear so hard that if he were alive, he wouldn't have been able to breathe.

I looked up at Mom to see if she had heard what Mel had said. Her face was impassive, so I don't think she heard anything. *Phew!* I was looking forward to lying out in the sun. I would have to do it when Mom wasn't around though, so I could do it at the beach. I can't wait to get down there! Soon, I will have never-ending summer!

***

"Turn left, arriving at your destination," the GPS voice droned.

"We're finally here!" Mom announced. We had turned into a little oasis. A pool on the left! A canal on the right! Condo, buildings scattered here and there. Palm trees everywhere! This was going to be the life! Oh, and did I mention a park, practically across the street from the group of condominiums!? This place was great!

"Look for building five," Mom told Mel and me. The two of us looked right and left, straining our necks until we spotted it. Building 5. It was the second building on the right.

We pulled into our parking spot, labeled number seven, and hopped out of the car.

"Grab a box, girls! Let's go see our new home," Mom chirped, as she got out of the car and popped open the trunk.

Mel pushed past her to grab the first box. On the side it was labeled, "Mel's Dolls." She stood by Mom, hopping up and down with excitement.

I grabbed a box with the words, "Taylor's Clothes" scribbled in permanent marker on its side.

Mom grabbed a box, too. We all walked up to the front door and Mom set down the box to find her key. She stuck it into the door's lock and as soon as it opened, Mel ran inside.

"Ha! I am the first in the house!" Mel squealed and ran up the stairs. Our condo was the upstairs one, so there were people living below us. Once you got inside there was a small place to leave your shoes, but nothing else before you reached the stairs that lead up to the actual condo. I walked past Mom and headed up the stairs after Mel. Mel went through the top entry door, and shut the door behind her.

"Open the door!" I demanded.

I didn't hear her coming, so I set down the box and opened the door. It was a big metal door that was painted white. It was very hard to open; I pushed and pulled and it hardly budged. After finally getting it opened wide enough, I saw a mechanism on the ceiling for keeping the door open and pulled it out and fastened the door to it. The door stayed put, so we wouldn't have to keep messing with opening it during this unloading process! Clever.

I picked the box back up and walked into the main area of the condo. The kitchen was on my left. Beyond the kitchen was a small living room. I turned left, to go around the kitchen into a mini hallway. To the right was a bathroom; straight ahead was what I assumed would be my room.

I wasn't sure, so I asked Mom, and she said that it was, indeed, my room. The master bedroom would be hers. (OF COURSE!) It was the biggest, so Mel and I should have gotten it! We are two and she is one, but whatever. Mom wouldn't be convinced otherwise.

I went into my new bedroom and began unpacking a few T-shirts, placing them into the dresser drawers. Then a thought hit me: we might not be keeping this furniture. Mom may sell it, so we could keep our own.

"Mom, are we keeping this furniture?" I asked.

"Well, I wasn't planning on it," she said. "But I kind of like it, now that I see it. It looks like it belongs in Florida, unlike our furniture. What do you think? Keep the chest, TV stand, and couch that was already here?"

"Yes. Let's keep the chairs on the lanai, the mirror in the living room, and the lamp on the kitchen table," I suggested. "Oh! Let's keep the table in the living room, too. It looks great!"

"Ok, so what are we doing with our furniture from Indiana?" Mom asked.

"We could sell it at a thrift store," Mel said, piping in from behind. She only knew what a thrift store was because our great-grandma was always shopping at them and sometimes took Mel along with her.

"Good idea, Mel! Now, how are we getting it there?" I asked. We could have the movers do it, but that would probably cost extra, if they even offered such a service in the first place.

"Some of the thrift stores have free pickup and delivery," Mom said, grabbing her phone out of her pocket to search the web. "Oh! I forgot we haven't had the Wi-Fi set up yet!" she moaned.

"One more thing added to our long list of things to do." I grumbled.

"What else do we have to do?" Mel asked, looking up at me.

"We have to dust, vacuum, scrub the tile in the kitchen, and repair the light in Mom's bathroom, etcetera!" I said, plopping myself down on the couch. Dust flew into the air and surrounded us. We all coughed, and Mel stuck her shirt over her mouth, before she ran into our bedroom, shutting the door.

Wow, they should have covered the couch with a sheet! Maybe we shouldn't keep the couch that was already here after all: it was really dusty, and I know I would be the one stuck cleaning it.

I looked over to Mom to see if she was set on the idea of keeping this couch. I could tell she was by the determination on her face.

I slowly stood up from the dusty couch and turned around to look at my back and butt. They were completely dust-covered! I really needed a shower anyways, especially now, so I shook myself off and went back out to the car to grab a few other things, like more clothes, my makeup, and a brush.

I took them all inside and pulled out an outfit to put on the closed toilet for when I got out of the shower. I stepped out of my clothes and into the shower. This was going to feel so good! I turned the handle and pulled it towards me. Nothing came out! Not a drop! I fumbled with it a few times, but gave up. It didn't work! I stepped back out, put my nasty, old clothes back on, and went to find Mom.

"I don't know, figure it out, you're not Mel's age anymore!" Mom exclaimed, when I questioned her.

"But Mom, I don't think the water is even on!" I retorted. "I would just be wasting my time if that is the case."

"I called, though! It has to be on," she snapped back at me. I huffed; just because she called to have the water turned on didn't mean that is had to be on. Anyone should know that.

"Mom, for some stupid reason the water isn't turning on! Call them back!" I yelled, getting frustrated. I felt gross from the drive and dusty from the couch. I really wanted my shower. "Please, just fix it!"

"I will call the plumber!" she, finally, said. "Surly, a plumber can fix this."

"Mom, the plumber isn't allowed to turn on the water meter!" I shrieked. "It's illegal! Only the water company can legally turn it on."

"It isn't the meter!" she yelled. She fumbled to grab her phone. She didn't know any plumbers down here. After realizing this, she let her shoulders slump and went down (without us) to the pool area to use the free WI-FI located there.

Was she really going to waste money just like that!? There were so many other things she could do first. Like she should call the water meter people and find out at least if they came, or if they hadn't been around yet, or when they would be.

Mom came back about fifteen minutes later. "I called a plumber. He'll be coming out tomorrow," she called out, as she walked through the door.

"He will just tell you the same thing I did," I said, rolling my eyes, not believing this could be happening.

I went into the kitchen next to look into the fridge. No light—that had to mean that the bulb was bad. *Add that to the growing list of things to fix.*

Then I looked in the freezer. My nose was assaulted with such a foul smell; I immediately had to plug my nose.

"Mom! We have another problem!" I yelled. There was mold on the whole inside of the freezer. There were also small packages of wrapped-up food and ice trays in the freezer, as well.

"Ahhhh! Yuck!" she exclaimed. "The people who used to live here left food in the freezer! The power has been out since they moved! How could they forget to clear out the freezer? Well, have fun with clearing that out, Sweetie."

"Wait a moment!" I cried after her, as she left the kitchen. "I am not cleaning this out! I will do everything else, but I refuse to clean up this mess! Enjoy." I slammed the freezer shut and turned around to walk away.

There was no way I was cleaning up this moldy mess. No thanks! She was the one that wanted this house in the first place. Would she seriously expect me to clean out that entire mold? Yuck! If so, she had lost her marbles. She could clean it herself.

"Come back here, young lady!" Mom shrieked. "I paid for this roof over our heads! I make the money! I pay for your education! I pay for the food you eat—" she yelled, but I cut her off.

Olympic Bound

"I fix your dinner," I countered. "I watch Mel. I pick her up from school. You sold my car! Just so we could move down here!"

Mom pinched the bridge of her nose and walked out of the room. I must have hit a nerve, because she was clearly frustrated and flustered.

I soon realized that if I don't want the freezer to look like World War III between beef and blueberries, I will have to clean it myself. If I don't do it, the freezer won't get any better. *How do you go about getting nasty mold out of a freezer anyway?* The power has been turned back on since we moved in, so my hands are going to freeze if I work on it as it is.

So, the only solution was to shut off the power. I warned Mom and Mel before I went to the fuse box to see what switch was the right one to flip. I experimented by turning off various switches until I came to the right one.

I started by pulling out the different moldy items. Most of them I couldn't tell what they where. I stared at them for a second, ignoring the smell, to guess what it was when it last looked edible—probably about six months ago. Chicken, maybe? Hard to tell. It was definitely some sort of meat, though.

I dumped it, along with a bag of frozen fruit, and one moldy, mystery item. The stench was almost too much to bear, but I tried my best to ignore it. Let me tell you, that was hard to do.

After every moldy container was in the trash, I washed my hands, tied the trash bag up, and took the trash downstairs, setting it on the patio outside. I made my way back upstairs and grabbed a butter knife to start scraping the mold from the roof of the freezer. It fell off into a pile on the floor of the freezer.

It was incredibly time consuming to scrape off the forest of mold with a butter knife, so I searched the house for something the past owners might have left behind that I could use as a more effective tool. To my surprise, I found a putty scraper in the cabinet under the sink.

I cheered, silently, in my head. *How lucky was that?* I dashed back to the freezer and started scraping off the blanket of mold.

I brushed the mold out into a Walmart bag and tied it up, putting it outside on the patio with the rest of the trash. Next, I used rags to wash the freezer with hand soap (since that was all I could find) and water. By the time I was done, the fridge looked great. Unfortunately, the smell stuck.

"Mom!" I called out. "Do we have anything to keep the freezer from smelling like rotting meat?"

Mom came out of her room with a spray bottle and handed it to me. I looked at the label. "Mom, this is kiwi hair spray," I handed the bottle back to her.

"It will make it smell nice." She proceeded to spray all six sides of the freezer.

I sniffed. *Now it smells like a mixture of rotting meat and strong, fruity hair spray. Not much of an improvement,* I thought.

Determined to get it done right, I rummaged through the kitchen some more. Under the sink, there were a gallon jug of vinegar and a large box of baking soda. That's when I remembered how Grandma used to clean everything using a mixture of those two things.

So I got to work making my own vinegar and baking soda paste to clean the freezer. I spackled in on, letting it sit for a little bit, and then wiped it away. I couldn't believe how well it worked! The smell was completely gone! Yay, Grandma! In that moment, I really missed her.

Pleased with myself, I closed the freezer door and turned the power back on, before starting to unpack the rest of my belongings.

I finished unpacking my clothes and then started on my books. My bookcase hadn't yet arrived, so I just stacked my book in piles on the floor, so I could get another box out of the way. As I was placing my last book on top of

KD Lee Writes

a pile, Mel screamed, and I turned around as quickly as possible and yelled out, "Mel?"

Chapter 5 – North Mangrove High

"What is it?!" I yelled. Mel stopped screaming. She was scooted halfway under her bed on her back.

"There is a huge spider," she said, in a hoarse whisper, before trying to pull herself out from under the bed. I pulled her by her feet until finally her head came free.

"How big is it?" I'm not afraid of spiders, but I definitely wanted to kill it before the thing could bite either of us in our sleep.

"Huge!" Mel demonstrated with her fingers how big. She spread her fingers apart about two and a half inches.

"That is with the length of its legs right?" I asked.

Mel nodded her head, eyes wide.

Wow, that is a big spider!

I took off one of my tennis shoes and gripped it in my right hand. Then, I dropped down on my belly to look for the culprit that scared my poor, little sister.

Finally, I saw it wedged in the corner. I scooted under the bed a bit and the spider started running along the wall. I swung my shoe, but it was kind of hard to do in this awkward position.

The monstrous spider changed course and moved away from the wall. I almost yelped, shocked by the speed of it! It paused. I saw my chance so I took it! I hit the spider before I squished it into the carpet, making sure it was absolutely dead.

Once I decided that the spider wasn't going to be moving any time soon, I lifted the shoe and picked up the spider by one of it's legs. I crawled back out from under the bed to show Mel that it wouldn't ever be able to hurt her at all.

***

Unpacking was an absolute pain. It took hours to make sure everything got from the moving van and the car into the little condo. Mom finally called the thrift shop and got the extra furniture out of the way. The next day the plumber came.

"Ma'am, it looks like your water's turned off," he drawled. "If you call the water company, they can send out someone to turn it on for you. I think they charge

$50 to turn it back on." He lifted his baseball cap and scratched his head.

Of course, Mom trusted the plumber and not me, her own daughter.

"Can't you do it?" Mom asked him.

"I could, but technically it is illegal, so I can't," he replied. "Only the water company employees can."

"Alright, thank you," she said. "How much do I owe you?"

"Well, since I didn't really help you out any, I'll just charge you for my gas, if that's alright," he offered.

"Sure, thanks!" Mom answered.

"That will be twenty dollars," he said. Mom opened her purse, fished out a twenty-dollar bill, she and handed it to the plumber.

"Have a good evening Ma'am," he said. He nodded at Mel and me before he left.

"See, if you had listened to me, then we wouldn't have had to pay that $20," I scolded Mom. "Now are you going to call the water company?"

"Okay," Mom said. "I admit I was wrong, but the water company is going to hear it from me! I was told that they had turned on my water. I even paid the $50 fee!"

"Well, can you trust me next time I tell you something?" I queried.

"It depends on what it is," she countered.

I rolled my eyes and grabbed Mel's hand, dragging her back to our room.

***

Today is Monday and we've gone a whole three days without water. I had to take a shower in my bathing suit down at the pool where they have a rinse-off shower. Mom went down with me to make sure I that didn't take a dip in the pool. She is way too paranoid.

Mel and I started school today, and I hadn't had a true shower since we left our old house; I was itching to get back to it. Mel loved it. She hated baths and showers, so this new development was awesome for her, except for the part of having to go to the bathroom in the pool house restroom. That was kind of a bummer, even for Mel.

But back to the subject of returning to school: I was a lot more nervous than Mel. It wasn't a great thing, starting school in the winter, especially if you were a high-schooler.

It probably wouldn't matter that much for Mel though, since she was just in third grade. I put on a cute outfit and found Mel in the kitchen eating cereal.

Olympic Bound

"Are you looking forward to ride the bus, today?" I asked her.

"I don't know anyone there yet; I wish you could drive me," Mel said, still staring at her cereal.

"But, Mel!" I said. "That is how you make friends, and you know I can't drive you to school even if I wanted to."

"I know," she said, gloomily.

I walked Mel up to the entry into the oasis and waited with her for her bus. Shortly after, she was on the bus and driving away. Then my bus arrived. I climbed up the few steps and tried to take a seat next to a girl in the middle of the bus, but she put her hand in my way.

"Sorry, I am saving this seat for someone," she said.

"That's ok." I walked down past a few more rows until I came across another empty seat.

"Is this seat taken?" I asked.

"Yeah, sorry," I rolled my eyes and walked back a little farther. There were a few more seats available in the back. A boy around my age sat alone in the back row closest to the window.

"This seat isn't taken," he said. I slipped off my backpack and set it in between my feet, after I sat down.

"Thanks," I said to him.

"Hey, no problem," he said. "Are you new? I don't remember seeing you around before." I nodded.

"Cool," he said. "So you got a name?"

"Taylor," I replied.

"I'm Harrison," he said. "So what year are you, junior, sophomore?"

"Sophomore."

"I'm a junior." Harrison had brown hair and brown eyes. Freckles speckled his nose and cheeks. He kept looking at me without saying anything, so I felt the need to say something to break the silence.

"So, have you lived here your whole life?" I asked.

"I lived in Georgia until I was four, but other than that, yeah," he answered.

There was more silence after that. I couldn't help but notice several people looking back at me and whispering to each other. To avoid the awkwardness, I grabbed a book from my backpack and started to skim through it.

After the bus picked up about five more kids, we finally arrived at North Mangrove High. I was thankful for the short bus ride.

Olympic Bound

The school was quite big, and I worried I wouldn't be able to find my class in time for the first bell. I rushed up to the main desk to get my schedule.

For the first period, I had history with Mrs. Baker. But before heading to my first classroom, I needed to find my locker to stuff a few things inside. I was glad to find my locker conveniently close by. I thought starting so late in the school year, all the convenient lockers would have been filled. Maybe someone moved away recently.

Closing my locker door, I stared down the long hallway. A girl brushed past me, and I stopped her. "Excuse me? Could you tell me where Mrs. Baker's class is?"

"Sure, I have advanced mathematics with Mr. Seg, which is just across the hall, so I can show you," she said.

"Thanks!" I followed her down the hall.

"So, you're a sophomore?" It was a rhetorical question, I realized, but I answered anyway.

"Yeah," I said. "Oh, my name is Taylor, by the way." She nodded.

"I'm Sophie, a senior," she informed me.

It didn't take long for us to reach Mrs. Baker's classroom.

"Here it is," Sophie said.

"Thanks," I replied. "See you around."

"Good luck with your first day," she said.

I disappeared inside the room for history class. There were a couple seats left in the middle, so I started walking toward them, before I got stopped by Mrs. Baker.

"You must be Taylor," she said, standing up from her desk. Her blonde hair hung down to the middle of her back, and she looked to be only thirty or so.

"Yeah, I am," I acknowledged.

She put a hand on each of my shoulders and spun me around to face the class. Almost all the faces were new except for a few people I had seen on the way in. I didn't know any of their names, however.

"Class, this is Taylor Reeve," Mrs. Baker introduced me. "She is new today. Everyone, say, 'Hi.'"

A few kids let out a half-hearted "Hi" or wave, looking bored.

Mrs. Baker released my shoulders, and I made my way to an empty desk. I sat down and Mrs. Baker started the lessons. It didn't take me long to catch up to the point where everyone else was. I've never have struggled when it comes to school.

Olympic Bound

***

At lunch, I sat with a group of girls my age. They were all chatting about boys, school, and the upcoming dance. Supposedly, it had been delayed because of a shortage of money to fund it. It was in two weeks.

"So how is your first day, new girl?" someone, I didn't know, asked. She had straight red hair and was super skinny.

"Ok, I guess," I respond.

"I'm Taffeta, by the way. That is Sam," Taffeta said, pointing to a plump, brunette girl sitting across from me.

"That's Jasmine, and that's Kate," Taffeta indicated. Jasmine was blonde and Kate was brunette, like Sam. I waved to them.

"This is my boyfriend, Chad, and that is Kate's boyfriend, Alex," Jasmine explained.

"I'm Taylor," I said to the group.

I wondered if it was a mistake sitting with them. They weren't really part of a *cool* group, if you know what I mean. But like anyone cooler than them would let a new girl like me sit with them anyways.

"Hey, Taylor, do you have a car?" Jasmine asked me.

I shook my head. "My mom . . . sold it," I said, a little embarrassed and not ready to get into that topic.

"Can she even do that?! I mean, it was your car right?" Jasmine pressed.

"Well, she gave it to me, but it was still in her name," I replied.

"She gave it to you? And then sold it?!" Jasmine continued to question.

"Yeah," I admitted.

"Well, that is too bad," Sam said. I nodded, in complete agreement with her.

"Why did she sell it anyway?" Alex asked.

"Uh, get a little extra cash for the move here," I clarified. Luckily, Taffeta changed the subject.

"Where are you from?" Taffeta asked.

"Indiana," I replied.

"Why did you move here?" Sam asked.

"Looking for endless summers. Have you been to Indiana?" I retorted, not really wanting to go into my whole life story.

"Hey, after school, do you want to go to the mall with us?" Taffeta asked.

"We could go in my car," Sam offered.

"Sure," I said, even though shopping wasn't my thing. These girls seemed nice enough, and it would be nice to make some friends.

***

Before my next period, I texted Mom to make sure it was alright to hang out at the mall after school. She promptly replied "OK". So, after school, the five of us drove to the mall. The first store we passed was an electronic store full of TVs and phones.

I recognized the movie playing on each of the TV screens. Daphne Dagan or Tiffany Dagan was playing the lead role. It was so hard to tell, since the two of them were identical twins.

Kate spotted the TV screens and started talking. "There is Daphne!" she said. "Did you guys watch the new episode of *Spliced Lives* last night?"

"Yes, and that's her sister, Tiffany, playing the lead role of that show," Jasmine informed us.

I spotted Harrison, with two other boys, eating at a little sandwich shop ahead of us. Taffeta spotted me looking at him and smirked.

"That's Harrison," she said knowingly.

"I know, I sat with him on the bus," I replied. All four of my new friends gasped.

"Really? That is *not* good!" they gasped in unison.

"Why?" I asked, wondering if he was some kind of mass murderer.

"He just broke up with his super-popular girlfriend, and she hasn't gotten over it," Kate said. "I bet she has already added you to her enemy list!"

"Or her arch enemy list," Sam added.

"We will watch your back," Taffeta offered.

Harrison spotted me and waved for me to come over.

I thought about it for a moment. Not wanting to be rude to him, I stood up and walked over to his table.

Harrison wiped his mouth with a napkin, bunched up the paper that his sandwich came in, and stood up to throw it in the trash.

"Hey, Taylor," he said, as I walked over to him.

Taffeta followed me. *Wow, she was serious about watching my back*, I thought.

"Hey," I said.

"This is Fred and he is Jerry," he said, introducing me to his two friends, who had just finished eating their sandwiches. They waved, taking a sip of their pops.

"Have you met, Taffeta?" I ask.

"Yeah, hey, Taffeta," he said to her.

She smiled slightly, before he turned his attention back to me. "Hey, Taylor, I was wondering if I could have your number?" Harrison asked. "I didn't get a chance to ask at school."

Taffeta eyed me, warningly. *But it would be rude to say no to him*, I thought.

"Sure, I don't have anything to write it on, though," I told him.

"That's ok, I'll just put it directly in my phone," he said and pulled out his phone.

I recited my number to him, and once he had it saved in his phone, he stuffed it back in his pocket. "Maybe I'll ask you out some time," he said.

"Ok," I replied lamely.

"Well, we got to get going, bye!" Taffeta said, abruptly, grabbing my arm and leading me away.

"Why did you give him your phone number!" she shouted, once we were out of ear shot.

"What was I supposed to say? 'No, you can't, because your ex might make my life miserable if I do?'" I implored her.

"Something like that anyway!" she snorted. "You could have told him you don't have a phone, just an iPod!"

"But he seems so sweet!" I admitted.

Taffeta shrugged. "Ok, but I won't enjoy saying I told you so."

That's when I saw it. The bathing suit in the window of Dick's Sporting Goods store. It was the style I was about to buy, before Dad passed away. It was on sale, as it was last years' model. I had enough cash in my purse to buy it...

Chapter 6 – Soaring High, Crashing Low

"Honey! Your phone's ringing!" Mom shouted from the other room. I rushed to see who it was. Weird. It was an unknown number.

I hit the answer button. "Hello?"

"Hey, Taylor, it's Harrison."

My face turned redder and my heart beat faster.

"Hey," I responded.

"So, I was wondering if . . . you would like to go on a date with me." Harrison stammered.

I thought about everything Taffeta and the girls had said to me about the situation.

After the briefest pause, I replied, "Sure, when?"

"Great!" he said. "What about Sunday? I'm busy on Friday and Saturday. Do you like mini putt-putt?"

"I've never done it before, but sure," I said.

"You've never played mini putt-putt?!" he exclaimed.

"Never," I said. "Anyway, what time?"

"How about five? We can go and eat somewhere afterward," Harrison said. "I'll pick you up; Taffeta told me you don't have a car anymore."

"She did?" I questioned.

"Yeah, so could you text me your address?" Harrison asked.

"Sure, ok," I said. "See you Saturday!" I hung up and thought about what Harrison had said. I wondered: *when did Taffeta talk to him?*

***

On the bus, the next morning, I questioned Taffeta. "You told Harrison I don't have a car?" I asked. "When were the two of you talking?"

"Look, he called me and asked me about you, ok?" She said.

"He did?" I asked. My heart started to beat a little faster again.

"Yes, I'm sorry," Taffeta apologized.

"No, it's ok," I replied. "I was just wondering when the two of you talked."

"So, did Harrison ask you out?" she asked.

"Yeah, so who was his girlfriend, anyway?" I asked.

Taffeta stiffened.

"What is it?" I asked.

"Um, it was Rebeca, the senior," she answered, but I could tell she was keeping something from me.

When we got to school, I tried to talk to Harrison multiple times, but the only time I saw him was outside of first period, at history class, and he was talking with his friends. I lost my courage to go up to talk to him. Instead, I went along to my next class.

At lunch, I sat with Taffeta and the rest of the group again. Taffeta didn't seem happy to see me.

"Hey, guys," I greeted them, taking the same seat as last time. They glared at me.

"What is it?" I asked

"Nothing," Jasmine replied. All of them looked down at their plates. I opened my water bottle.

"Come on!" I said. "Something is obviously bothering you. What did I do?" None of the girls responded.

"Taffeta, this is ridiculous," Sam exclaimed. "Just tell her, already!"

"I like Harrison, ok?" Taffeta, finally said. "We made up that stuff about his ex-girlfriend."

This actually didn't surprise me.

"Well, I'm not canceling the date if that is what you want," I told her, taking a bite of my pizza.

"I didn't think you would," she said. Taffeta hesitated, as though she was about to go on, but she didn't. Instead she opened up her Jell-O and scooped some of the jiggly stuff into her mouth.

The rest of lunch was extremely awkward, and I couldn't wait until classes started. I bet I was not the only one that was thinking that.

***

I climbed down the few steps to get off the bus and raced up to the condo. I wished I had an umbrella, because it was pouring rain outside. When I looked out to our parking lot, I noticed Mom's car wasn't home, yet. She was probably still in an interview for a job at Palm Estates Reality. She had told me she was going there.

Olympic Bound

Turned out the job that Mom thought she had filled before we moved to Florida got taken. They had just recently called her to inform her of the bad news. Now, Mom was out of work, which wouldn't help our situation any.

So, while I waited, I did my algebra homework and then started in on my history paper. If I had a car, I would have driven to the library and picked up some books, but it looked like that wasn't happening until Mom got back with the car.

The door opened and I swiveled around. Mom stood in the doorway, dripping wet.

"So, how did the interview go?" I asked her.

She frowned and shrugged. That meant she didn't get the job.

I thought of all the things I could say about how moving to Florida without a job already locked in for certain was stupid, among other things. She looked so depressed that I didn't want to get into an argument with her. So, I kept my mouth shut.

"What office are you going to try, next?" I asked.

"I have another interview scheduled for tomorrow. Cross your fingers for me," Mom said, plopping down on the couch. She pulled a cigarette out of her pocket and I dashed over to snatch it from her before she could light it.

"Mom!" I exclaimed. "You haven't smoked in two years!" I said.

Mom made a grab for the smoke.

"Actually I haven't had a cigarette in five minutes; now give that back," she growled.

"What!" I cried, frustrated. "How long have you been smoking?"

"Since we moved," she said and pulled another cig from her purse. She plopped it in her mouth and flicked a lighter to ignite the end. I refrained from taking the second one and instead gave her a disappointed look. Sometimes I forgot which one of us was the mother and which one of us was the child.

"I'm sorry, ok, but why do you care anyway?" she asked.

Second and third hand smoke is why I care, I thought. But we had been over this before so I just rolled my eyes, grabbed my homework, and stormed off to my room. I slammed the door shut.

Mel finally got home around 4:30 P.M., after I had finished making dinner. Once the three of us had eaten our meal, Mel asked me for a favor.

"Taylor could you drive me to the library?" She asked. "I need to get a book on acting. My teacher is having us do a report on what we want to be when we are older, and I want to be an actress. Please?"

I nodded that I would. I wanted to go to the library, too, so this would give Mom a reason to let us borrow her car.

Mel worked on Mom next and got her to agree fairly quickly. The two of us went out to the car and Mel (again) sat in the front passenger seat.

"Please, please can I sit in the front just one time?!" She begged. I hesitated for a moment, but decided to let her sit in front, just this once. She was only eight though. Legally, she was old enough in Florida to sit in the front seat, but the suggested guidelines are to sit in the back seat until you are 4'9" tall and thirteen years old. Hopefully, I won't get pulled over. Mel is still so young and small.

She thanked me multiple times while I looked up directions to the library on my phone.

"Thank you, thank you, and thank you!" She pulled on her seatbelt and sat back, grinning from ear to ear.

Soon, we were on the way. "How far is it?" Mel asked, anxiously. She may like reading even more than I do.

"About fifteen minutes away," I answered. I turned on the radio and Taylor Swift music blared from the speakers. I took my eyes off the road for a split second to look at a big house to my left.

"Taylor!" Mel screamed.

I snapped by head back to the road only to see a big semi-truck pull out in front of me. I slammed on the brakes. It was as if time was moving through molasses. The truck was right in front of me and the car wouldn't stop fast enough.

The first thing I thought of was Mel. *Why had I agreed to let her sit in the front seat?* I threw my arm in front of her to protect her from the airbag before it deployed. We crunched into the truck and all of Mom's junk that she had left in the car flew everywhere.

The semi had hit us so hard, our car had spun around before coming to a stop. Despite being disoriented, I looked over at Mel. She lay motionless with her head hanging down.

"Mel?" I shook her, gently. She remained motionless. That was when I noticed a pencil stuck in her stomach. *How did that get there?*

"Mel!" I screamed. I put two fingers to her neck to check her pulse. It was beating slowly and faintly beneath my fingers. I sighed in relief, but she didn't look good. There was a streak of blood running down her face from where her head had smacked into the passenger window. Just then, I heard a knocking sound. The driver of the semi attempted to open my door.

"Are you, ok?! Oh, my God. What have I done?" He stared past me at Mel, gripping his head.

"Did you call 911?" I asked him.

He nodded, furiously.

"Don't just stand there, help her!" I screamed at him, even though I realized there wasn't much he could do. He scurried around to her side and opened the passenger door.

He unbuckled her seat belt and gingerly lifted her out of her seat. She stayed limp in his arms, as he laid her down on the road. He took off his shirt and held it against her head where she was bleeding the most.

I moved to unbuckle my seatbelt, but the movement caused a shooting pain to course through my body. My ribcage felt majorly injured from the airbag. I had never broken a bone before, so I wasn't sure if the severe pain I was feeling was a broken rib or just bruised. Plus, my head felt like it was going to split apart from the impact.

I managed to get my seatbelt unlatched, and I fell out of the car. I staggered as best as I was able, in my current condition, over to kneel down next to Mel. She was not moving and still unconscious.

I stroked Mel's hair and started crying.

Glaring at the truck driver, I sobbed, "What were you doing? Were you sleeping at the wheel?! You ran a red light!"

I must have looked hysterical. Wet tears flowed down my face.

He stuttered, trying to think of what to say, tears in his eyes, too.

I turned back to Mel and stroked her hair some more with my right hand, while I held the shirt against her head with my left hand.

I shouldn't have let her sit in the front seat! I should have paid more attention to the road! There were many ways I could blame myself for this, but I chose to not keep dwelling on these events I couldn't change. Instead, I focused on the task at hand.

"It will be alright," I told Mel, choking on my tears. I had no way of knowing that. It was more wishful thinking.

A random stranger—a Good Samaritan—parked by us and rushed over to help, but there wasn't anything she could do. After what seemed like ages, I finally heard sirens in the distance. Tears of relief flowed down my face when not just one ambulance, but two arrived along with multiple police vehicles.

Olympic Bound

The traffic, that got backed, up after the wreck, moved out of the way. Mel's eyes flickered open, and she wailed in pain. It killed me to see her like this.

"It hurts," she mumbled, weakly.

I cried with relief that she was at least present enough to feel the pain and speak of it.

KD Lee Writes

Chapter 7 – The Longest Night

Mel and I were forced to get into different ambulances. I insisted that I was fine and that I could ride with her, but apparently my complexion said otherwise. There was no hiding my injuries, let alone my pain. I finally stopped arguing with the paramedics and agreed to be loaded into the ambulance on a stretcher.

All I could think about while they bandaged up different parts of my body was Mel. "She will be ok, right?" I asked to no one in particular.

The woman that was working on my arm answered honestly. "I don't know, Honey, but I have seen people survive worse," she said.

I tried to nod, but my neck was too stiff; it was painful to move an inch.

Finally, we were at the hospital and a team of doctors and nurses whisked me off to my own hospital room. All the while, they asked me questions about my identity. They must have called my mom, because soon after, she was in my hospital room.

"Tell them I am fine, let me see Mel!" I begged her.

She sadly shook her head.

"You are more injured than you think," she said gently. "But you're in better condition than Mel. I'm sorry, but I am going to have to leave you to go back to her room. Stay here. Please rest. You are going to be ok. I just wanted to make, sure for myself, before leaving you alone to be with Mel."

Tears filled her eyes, but she stubbornly kept them from flowing down her cheeks. She left the room, and I decided that I was not going to just sit around. I sat up, and the nurses and a doctor hurried over to quiet me and hold me down.

"You have just been in a very traumatic wreck," the doctor told me. "You may have broken ribs, and you are suffering from a minor concussion."

"Just let me see Mel!" I shouted at him, despite the stabbing pains in my chest from where the airbag had bruised me. The doctor kept his hands planted firmly on my wrists as I struggled to sit up.

"You need to remain still," he insisted. "We have to run some more tests on you."

I let out an angry cry before lying back down. Suddenly, I was too tired to struggle. Covering my face with one hand, I began to sob.

This is my entire fault, and now Mel might die because of me, I thought. I had already lost Dad; could Mom and I survive after losing another person we love? It just didn't seem like I would be able to carry on after such a terrible loss.

The doctors seemed to image me from head to toe, before poking and prodding me, verifying my injuries were minor.

Nurses traveled in and out of my room throughout the night, monitoring this, testing that, but none of them would tell me anything about Mel. Mom didn't even visit again, which worried me.

***

I fell in and out of sleep all night. Still, no Mom. No one would let me know how Mel was doing. Nurses would randomly walk by and at this point, rarely checked on me.

***

I woke up with the sun peeking through my hospital window. It was morning! *Where is Mom?*

I looked to the doorway and saw Mom standing there, wringing her hands, and staring at me with blood-shot eyes. Seeing me wake up, she came into my room.

I sat up quickly, which I realized was a mistake on my part, because my chest and head started aching again. Even my back was unbelievably sore. I had always thought of myself as having a high pain tolerance, but this agony was leaving me down for the count. I fought past tears of discomfort to talk to Mom.

"Is Mel, ok?" I asked.

Mom shook her head, as she slowly sat down on the edge of my bed. Now tears were leaving salty streaks down her cheeks.

"Mom?" I asked.

"She didn't survive the night, Taylor," Mom whispered.

In that moment, time stopped. I gasped in horror; it just sounded like a cross between a whimper and a cry.

Mom hugged me, and I hugged her as tightly as I could. Her hug was hurting me so much, but I easily ignored the pain. The pain in my heart was overwhelmingly more so. I was bawling so hard that I struggled to breathe. After about twenty minutes of just Mom and me hugging and crying together, I managed to choke out a sentence.

"When? When was it that it happened?" I asked her. It was hard to get the words out.

"A little after midnight... it... I... well it just took some time to work up the courage to tell you," she said.

I didn't say anything in return. I just continued sobbing on her shoulder, while she cried on mine.

"It's my fault, I shouldn't have let her sit in the front seat," I admitted.

Mom hugged me tighter. "It isn't your fault, it is the truck driver's fault," Mom explained. "He is the one who ran the red light. It sounds like he fell asleep."

I don't know who told her about the truck driver, but I still felt like it was my fault. In some ways, I knew it was.

"Did she say anything before she died?" I asked.

I was surprised Mom could even make out what I asked though all my tears.

"Yes, she told me to thank you for letting her sit in the front seat," Mom whimpered.

I let out a muffed cry, covered my mouth and collapsed into my Mom's shoulder again.

***

After a couple days in the hospital, I was finally well enough to be released. I found myself thinking of what

Mel would have looked like or done as an adult. Now I would never know. Mom wasn't doing any better.

She forced herself to go to a job interview, since we were starting to hurt for money. In a moment of extreme sadness, I pulled out the swimsuit I had secretly purchased at the mall, after my first outing with the girls and talking with Harrison. I slipped it on.

Swimming used to be my stress reliever. Now, I needed a stress reliever more than ever. I walked down to the pool with a towel wrapped around me. It was only a few condos down.

I pulled the towel off my shoulders and jumped into the deep end. Water closed in around me, and I felt a pulse of adrenaline. As I sank down to the bottom of the pool, memories of Dad and Mel came rushing back to me. I wanted to break down and cry, but I didn't.

Instead, I hit the bottom of the deep end and pondered my loss in the silence of the deep water. Running out of air, I instinctively propelled myself up with my feet. As I exploded up through the smooth surface of the water, the air felt foreign to me at first. Instinct took over, my lunges expanded with a deep breath, and I began to swim. I swam a couple laps. Every once in a while, I looked up at the clock that hung above the pool house doors to make sure I didn't stay too long. I didn't want to find out what Mom would do if she caught me swimming.

After the crash and not swimming for so long, my muscles ached with each stroke I took. Finally, I stopped swimming and pulled myself up out of the pool. I wrapped myself in my towel and hurried up to the condo.

My whole body ached in ways I didn't know it could. I decided to take a hot shower. It was hard to leave the hot water of the shower, as it eased my bruised and aching muscles.

After toweling off quickly, I dressed in cozy clothes and sat down on the couch to wait for Mom to come home.

A few minutes of waiting, and I heard her car pull up, the door shut, and her keys jingled in the lock.

"Hello, Honey!" she said, as she walked through the door.

"Did you get the job?" I asked, trying to make an effort not to sound as depressed as I felt. The pool had helped, though. Actually, if I was honest with myself, it helped a lot.

"Yes! You are now looking at an employee for Sun Chaser Reality!" she said proudly.

I don't know how she managed so much enthusiasm, but I tried to mimic it.

"Great!" I said, but my heart just wasn't in it.

"It might be that she was just feeling sorry for me," Mom admitted. "I did break down in tears and told her everything about Mel and how we are hurting for money, but it doesn't matter, I still got the job!" She did a little victory dance on the way to her room and closed the door.

***

That night, for the first time since Dad died, Mom made dinner. I didn't touch it, however. I was too depressed to be hungry.

"Come on, my cooking isn't that bad," Mom encouraged.

In that moment, I could tell that she was trying to be strong and cheerful for me. This time, I couldn't do the same for her. I had lost too much, and I felt responsible for everything that had happened to us.

"It isn't that," I said, even though she already knew that.

"You have got to stop moping, Taylor. Get on with your life. You are going back to school on Monday, after the funeral," Mom said with finality.

The thought of school hadn't even crossed my mind. I didn't reply to her, but I knew I was not going to school on Monday. That was a fact. It was funny, too. It was strange to me that after Dad's death, Mom just mopped around and cried, yet after Mel's death, Mom had

Olympic Bound

reassumed her position as Mom. Now I was the one moping around and doing nothing but cry. At least I was not drinking or smoking.

Chapter 8 – A Whole New Level of Torture

Sun rays peeked through the curtain of my bedroom window. It felt weird not to have Mel snoring in the bed next to me. I got up and ran my fingers along the quilt covering her mattress. Mom had made the bed after we got back from the hospital.

I don't know why she bothered, but she did; so, it sat empty and neat all by itself in the corner. I pulled back the sheets and the quilt and climbed in, breathing in the smell of vanilla shampoo. It was so perfectly Mel.

I cried softly into her fluffy pillow. Finally, I remade the bed, so Mom wouldn't notice, and made my way to the kitchen. It was Sunday. Tomorrow I would have to argue with Mom about school, and she would be late for work because of it.

After not eating much for so long, I finally gave in to hunger. I pulled a bowl out of the cabinet followed by milk, cereal, and a spoon. After filling the bottom of the bowl with cereal and milk, I put them both away, sticking a spoon full of purple swirl cereal into my mouth. It tasted like blueberries, blackberries, and sugar.

Mom chose that moment to come into the room to get her cereal out. She ate plain Cheerios. I liked the Honey Oat Cheerios kind the best, but the plain ones were good, too.

"Taylor, it's good to see you eating something," she said.

I was tempted to push the food back away from me, but ignored the temptation, knowing Mom would be disappointed.

"Are you ready for school tomorrow? I called to tell them you will be back tomorrow," she declared.

I shrugged.

"You are going no matter what you say to me," she warned. "I understand that it must be very hard for you. The two of you were very close and for some reason you have gotten it into your head that you are to blame, *which you aren't*. But you can't let depression and sadness come between you and a good future. You think it is easy for me? I haven't had one drink since Mel's death, not one!"

"Hurrah, hurrah," I said, lamely. "But you did smoke, and that is worse."

Mom pursed her lips, and I could tell she was about to say something she would regret later. She must have thought better of it, because she stopped herself. That was the thing about Mom. She had to have a distraction whenever something terrible happened. When Dad died it was alcohol, now it was smoking.

"My point is that I am going to work to help us cope," Mom said. "Will you go to school for you? Not for me, but for you? You of all people know how important a good education is."

I stuffed another bite of cereal into my mouth. I was not in the mood to talk right now. If I wanted to stay home and mope, I would stay home and mope.

"Taylor?" Mom asked.

"Shut up, ok?! Get off my back!" I screamed. "You may be able to go to work and not even care about what happened to Mel. But I do, and it is my fault she isn't going to school tomorrow. It is my entire fault she isn't going to college, getting married, having kids, growing old, or meeting her grandkids!" Tears stained my face, making my eyes burn.

"How can you say that?" Mom said, aghast. "I do care about her! It is very hard for me not to just lay in bed and cry, but I am working hard and not drinking for you! And Taylor, it isn't your fault she isn't here! Get that thought out of your thick skull! You didn't do anything wrong! It's not your fault the truck driver fell asleep at the wheel and ran that red-light! So just go to school for me, so I know I am doing something right!"

I got up, abandoning my now soggy cereal, and raced to my room, slamming the door behind me.

I couldn't hear Mom crying outside since I was crying so hard myself. I didn't need to hear her to know she was crying anyways. I should have felt guilty for yelling at her, but I didn't. She shouldn't make me go to school yet. It was only one day since the funeral. That would be so harsh.

***

Mom had dealt with the all funeral planning, so I didn't know what to expect. Despite this, I was still caught off guard when I saw the casket was closed. I had to see Mel again before it was too late.

"Mom, why is the casket closed?" I asked.

"They do that when… the body doesn't look the same as it did before it died," she answered.

I didn't like how she referred to Mel as a body, like she was an inanimate object instead of a person.

"But I'll get to see her again before she is buried right?" I asked.

"No, it stays closed now," Mom said.

Not many people had arrived yet, so I felt tempted to brush off the flowers and see Mel one last time.

I imagined what she would look like if I did: Mel would look pale. All the blood that was on her last time I saw her, would be cleaned off, and her clothes would be clean. Her hair would be lying around her shoulders. Mel hated it down like that, though. She always wore it in a ponytail.

I will never see her again, I realized in horror. Sure, I'd see pictures again, but I would never see the *real* Mel again. Not that that lifeless corpse in that casket was Mel, it, like the pictures, was just a memory of her. The real girl, my beautiful, smart and sarcastic sister was gone.

I didn't cry during the funeral. All my tears had already been shed. I just sat catatonically in the front row, listening to the preacher talk about my delicate, little sister as if he knew her.

It made me mad that he talked about her like she was gone forever. Logically, I knew she was, but it was easier just to pretend that she was on a long vacation and would be coming back. Eventually.

It was easier to pretend that I was not the cause of her death. It was easier to think that I would get to see her grow up and go to each one of her still to come birthdays, help set up her graduation party, be the maid of honor at her wedding. But in reality, I really would never see her again. My little sister was gone forever, all because of me.

***

The two of us got home, only to almost jump out of our skins, as the doorbell rang soon after we'd walked through the door. Mom went downstairs to answer it.

"Hello, is Taylor here?" the person at the door asked.

"And who are you?" Mom questioned in return.

"Oh, sorry," the visitor said. I still couldn't place the voice. "I'm Harrison. I'm taking Taylor to go play mini golf."

"Taylor!" Mom called out, "Your friend, Harrison is here!"

Harrison! I had totally forgotten about our date! I knew what Mom was doing; she was trying to get me out of the house. I came to the door and Harrison looked me up and down. I realized that I was still dressed in all black clothing from the funeral.

"I was just at a funeral," I murmured. "My, sister died. Sorry, I didn't call you. I've been out of sorts. Sorry," I mumbled.

"Oh, no!" Harrison said. "I am sorry. I realized that you weren't at school, but I didn't know why. We don't have to go if you don't want, I would totally understand." Harrison was being so sweet, and I didn't really want to stand him up. But on the other hand, I really didn't feel like mini golf or going out to eat.

"Maybe we could go next weekend, would that be alright?" I asked.

"Yeah, that's fine," he replied. "Don't worry about it, I get it."

"Would you like to come inside?" Mom asked from behind me.

Harrison shook his head. "That's alright Ma'am," he said. "I think I'll go home. I am sorry about your sister, Taylor."

Once Harrison left, I closed the door and disappeared up into my room.

Not only had I let my sister down, but I had let Harrison down, too. Was I cursed? Was I destined to have all happiness disintegrate? Am I just prone to bad luck?

***

The next morning, Mom insisted that I go to school, but she couldn't get me out of bed. She finally gave up and left for work. I stayed in bed until noon, before I finally got up and made some eggs.

Mel liked her eggs with lots of pepper, so I covered mine with it even though I didn't really like it that much. I just wanted to feel close to her. Not like that helped much, it just made my mouth burn.

Around four in the afternoon, Jasmine stopped by the condo. When I answered the door, she immediately apologized for not calling before coming past.

"Are you alright?" Jasmine asked. I shook my head. No I was not alright. She hugged me tightly.

"I am so sorry, I just had to stop by to see how you were doing," she said.

"Wait, how do you know about my sister?" I asked.

"That is another reason I came," she said. "I needed to warn you. Everyone at school knows what happened. There is this website www.crazydisastersinflorida.com, and there is a video of the car crash and you, like, crying over your sister."

"What!?" I exclaimed.

She nodded, sympathetically.

Olympic Bound

"Come on in if you want," I said. "I'm going to take a look at this website."

"Are you sure you want to do that?" she asked. "I mean; won't it be hard seeing your sister like that again?"

I turned, and she followed me inside. We made our way upstairs, and I pulled out Mom's computer. Sure enough, under LOCAL DISASTERS, I was the first one on the list.

A Car Crash from Hell

Sixteen-year-old Taylor Reeve and eight-year-old Melody Reeve (sisters and new residents of Fort Myers, Florida) were on their way to the library when the driver of a semi-truck fell asleep and ran a red light.

Taylor, who was behind the wheel, slammed on the brakes, but the car couldn't stop fast enough. The two girls smashed into the truck's side.

Both of the girls smacked their heads upon impact, causing concussions. But that wasn't the worst of it. When Melody's airbag deployed, the impact crushed her ribs and face and impaled her abdomen with a pencil!

KD Lee Writes

The trucker, along with many strangers that saw the accident, called 911 and soon authorities arrived on the scene. The two sisters were separated into two ambulances and rushed to a nearby hospital. Unfortunately, Melody didn't survive the night.

Luckily, Taylor Reeve got away with only scratches, a minor concussion, a little bruising from the airbag, and a bit of whiplash.

Taylor's mother is planning on suing the trucker's trucking company.

I was digging deeper into the story when I found that this is not the first tragedy for the Reeve family. Not only is Taylor's mother a recovering alcoholic, but I also found that Taylor's dad, Tomas Reeve, drowned after being caught in a riptide while swimming at the beach during a vacation. Hopefully, Taylor and her mother will have better luck in the future!

Watch video below to see the crash first hand.

I scrolled down and pressed play. The crash looked just as bad as I expected. I saw the trucker's frightened expression as knelt close to Mel's limp body.

I also saw me sobbing pitifully over her body. Great, now everyone would be awkward around me because they would not be sure what to say. I read a section of the article over again. Mom was planning on suing? She hadn't told me that.

I knew she was looking for insurance money to buy a new car and pay for the rental she got after I crashed her car, but suing? That was news to me.

"It's on YouTube, too, and in the newspaper, and on the news. Actually, I bet you are on Wink News at 5," Jasmine added.

Super! Not only would all the kids at school know, but so would everyone in Florida. So not cool.

"Thanks for your warning, Jasmine," I said. I was glad that she had come over to tell me this.

"No problem, Taylor, what are friends for?" she replied.

Chapter 9 – Relief

School pretty much sucked to the greatest extent. Everyone looked at me, but when I looked in someone's direction, they would go back to whatever they were doing. Some checked on how I was holding up and others just opened their mouth to say something, but would end up changing their minds and kept silent.

It was pretty gruesome, but every evening while Mom worked, I swam, getting faster and faster. Now, I could swim down and back—one lap— in 11 seconds. Five seconds down, one second doing the turnaround and five seconds back.

I was also beginning to master the flip to turn around. I used to be really good, but after not practicing for so long, it was a little difficult to do it fast.

I practiced like I had never before. It was the only time I could forget the hell I was in. When I swam, not only did I get a break from the pain, but I felt exhilarated and maybe even happy. When I swam, I could hear Dad cheering and my little sister urging me on. Just like the good old days: I wanted to bring home a trophy to give to my baby sister. Her eyes had always lit up when I won.

I had to swim.

It was my only escape.

***

Before I knew it, it was Sunday again and Harrison was taking me to play mini golf. To be honest, I was surprised he even showed up. I couldn't believe he even wanted to hang out with me! I hadn't exactly been pleasant to be around, lately.

"I'm really sorry to hear about your sister," Harrison repeated. When we walked to the door, I could tell he was uncomfortable and was trying to think of polite things to say.

"You don't have to tip-toe around me just because my sister died," I said. "I'm determined to have some fun today instead of just sitting at home missing her and feeling sorry for myself."

"I'm not tip-toeing around you," Harrison exclaimed bluntly.

"Uh, huh, so after mini-golf, where are we going to eat?" I asked, changing the subject.

Olympic Bound

"I was thinking about Sunset Diner, have you ever eaten there?" he asked. "They have the best fries."

"I haven't," I said. "That sounds great."

***

We pulled into the parking lot of the mini-golf course. Harrison opened the door for me, and we walked up to the pay booth.

The whole place was decorated in a pirate theme. There was even a pirate ship that you had to walk through to play one of the holes.

"Two rounds, please," Harrison said to the man behind the desk.

"Harrison!" the man said, "So good to see you again. It's been a while! Go ahead and pick out your clubs and golf balls."

I picked out a club and a pink ball, pink was Mel's favorite color, though I normally prefer blue. Harrison picked out a green ball.

"Do you want any snacks or drinks?" Harrison asked. I noticed that there were many unhealthy choices, both to eat and drink.

"No thanks," I said.

Harrison thanked the man at the counter, and then we walked over to the first hole. I looked over to the moat to my right. There was a little slab of an island covered in baby alligator statues.

"Wow, those alligator statues look so realistic!" I exclaimed.

"Don't freak out, but those aren't statues," he said.

"Really?" I asked. "Awesome! Why did you think I would freak out?"

"Because some girls I know would," he answered.

"Well, I guess I am not like some girls," I countered.

I spotted an alligator-feeding machine and dug a quarter out of my pocket to get some food for the animals.

Once I had a handful, I handed half of the food to Harrison. He took it and threw some in. Only one of the alligators went after it. So, I threw some closer to the smallest alligator. But by then, the little alligator must have had enough sun, as it slipped into the water.

I went ahead and threw in the rest of the food. None of the other alligators moved. "I guess they're not hungry," I said, clapping my hands together to get the dust off.

"Do you want to hit first?" Harrison asked.

Olympic Bound

"Go ahead," I offered.

I watched him closely since I had never hit a golf ball in my life. He crouched down behind the ball and got his line. First, he needed to hit the ball into an "alligator's" mouth. Then the ball would, hopefully, roll down a tunnel to the green at the bottom of the stairs.

Harrison stood up to the ball and hit it lighter than I anticipated. The ball rolled up to the alligator, barely missing its teeth that were blocking the way and rolled into the tunnel.

"Yeah!" He cheered. He moved out of the way, so I could set my ball down.

I lined up like Harrison had, and then I hit the ball. It rolled... would it make it? Nope... it smacked right into the fake epoxy-resin alligator's teeth and rolled all the way back to where it started at my feet. Gosh. This was going to be harder then I originally thought.

I repositioned my feet before I hit it again. This time, it rolled up... and hit the teeth again. I sighed in exasperation.

I lined up again, saying in my head: *third time is a charm.* I hit the ball and it rolled right into the gap between teeth and disappeared into the tunnel. Harrison gave me a high-five, and then we descended the stairs to where our two golf balls sat waiting for us.

Harrison took the next shot. He was still about six feet from the hole and there was a small mound in the way. Somehow, he managed to hit the next one in.

"Nice shot!" I told him, standing up next to my ball that was about two feet from where Harrison's was. I hit the ball and it flew off the face of my club and passed the hole, bouncing into the brick barrier behind it. Luckily, I made the next shot.

***

After mini-golf, Harrison and I drove to the diner.

"So your mom never lets you swim? Ever?" he asked, after I told him everything the article didn't mention.

"Nope," I said. "She's afraid that I'll drown, too, despite the fact that I'm such a great swimmer! I used to want to go to the Olympics. I still do. Wait a second, I have an idea! After we eat, let's go to the YMCA! Do you swim?" I asked him.

"Uh, not really. I can swim, but I don't normally," he said.

"You want to?" I asked. "Oh, shoot! My swimsuit is at home and so is my Mom. Maybe we could stop by the mall, and I could get a new one!"

Harrison didn't seem very excited about the plan.

"Well, I would get to see you in a bikini," he contemplated.

I rolled my eyes. He is such a boy.

"I'm in," he decided. I smiled.

Once we were almost done with our hamburgers and fries, I texted Mom to tell her we had decided to go to a movie.

Me: *Is it ok if Harrison and I go to the movies?*

She texted back right away.

Mom: *Sure have fun! Make sure you're home by 10:30.*

Me: *K*

She's probably glad I am not staying home, sulking, I reasoned, feeling a little guilty about lying to my mom.

I stuck the phone back in my pocket, and we drove to the mall. I tried on three swimsuits before I found one that fit me. Next, Harrison and I planned to go to his house to pick up his swimsuit.

"Are you sure we should do this?" Harrison asked. "You know, since your mom is kind of against you swimming?"

"It isn't like we are drinking or doing something illegal," I replied. "She's just unreasonably paranoid. Let's go!"

I turned on the radio and rap music came blaring out of the speakers. I changed the station. The next station was county. Great . . . rap and country, my least favorite music genres. I tried another station, but all I got was a static-filled commercial.

"Try 98.1 or 96.9," Harrison suggested. "They have some good music."

"Thanks," I said. "I'm not used to the radio stations down here, yet." I tried 96.9 and a modern hit spilled out of the speakers.

"Is this song, ok?" I asked Harrison.

He nodded.

"Cool," I said.

An awkward silent moment passed between us before Harrison spoke again. "So how long has it been since you swam?" he asked.

"Right after I got out of the hospital, I needed a major stress reducer," I explained. "The only thing that has helped me feel any close to better has been swimming. Mom was at a job interview, so I went down to the pool by my place."

"So you still swim quite a bit then, or not?" he asked.

"That was the first time I've swum since my dad died," I replied somberly.

"Oh," Harrison murmured.

I could tell that he didn't know how to answer that. We let the conversation drop. Soon we pulled into his driveway. Harrison didn't live in a condo like Mom, Mel . . . I mean Mom and me. He had a good-size house with a two-acre yard in a nice neighborhood.

"I must warn you, my parents are home and they are a little, well, overprotective," Harrison admitted.

"I bet they aren't as bad as my mom," I replied. "She won't even let me in a pool, remember?"

"Just warning you, ok?" Harrison said. "And I have a little brother and sister, too. My sister isn't home, but my brother is, and he is kind of a pain in the butt."

"Do you want me to wait in the car?" I asked. "I mean; you are just running in to grab a swimsuit."

"No, my family will just ask me to bring you in so they can meet you anyway," he said. "Ready?"

"I guess?" I replied, unsure.

The two of us walked up to the front door, and Harrison opened it. Inside, the place was spick and span. There wasn't a speck of dust on anything.

As if reading my mind, Harrison explained apologetically, "They're kind of clean freaks."

A woman in her late forties or early fifties peeked her head into the sitting room where we were standing. She was wearing an apron and had her hair back in a tight bun that looked like it would rip the skin right off of her head. I wondered how she got it that tight! There wasn't a hair out of place, either. Her hair was brown with streaks of gray. She wiped her hands on her apron, even though it looked like her hands were already clean.

"Harrison, I wish you would have told me you were bringing company," she said. "I would have straightened myself up a bit!"

Harrison rolled his eyes.

"Mom, you look fine," he said, kissing her on the cheek.

"So who is your new friend?" she asked.

"Mom, this is Taylor," Harrison said. "She is the one who just moved here. Taylor, this is my mom, Ruth"

"Hello, it is very nice to meet you," I said, and I shook her hand.

"It is very nice to meet you, too!" she replied. "I'm truly very sorry about your sister, too. You poor dear!"

A lump caught in my throat. News traveled fast. I guess Harrison must have told her. Or possibly she heard it on the news. Just then, a man, who I assumed was Harrison's dad, came around the corner.

Olympic Bound

I introduced myself to him.

"Nice to meet you. I am Mr. Fuller. You can call me Steve. Hey, I thought you two were playing mini-golf and going out to eat," Harrison's dad said to both of us.

"We did," Harrison replied. "Now we're going to swim at the YMCA. We just stopped by so I could pick up my swimsuit."

Next, Harrison's brother came flying into the room. He looked like he was about a year younger than Mel when she... she... nothing, never mind.

"And this is my brother, Peter," Harrison said. "Peter, this is Taylor."

I waved at him.

His brother shouted, "Harrison's got a girlfriend! Harrison's got a girlfriend! Taylor and Harrison sitting in a tree K-I-S..."

Ruth stopped Peter mid-song. I looked over at Harrison and his cheeks were bright red.

"Leave your brother alone, Peter," Ruth said. Peter ran right back upstairs after his mother admonished him.

"I'll go get my swimsuit," Harrison added, quickly. "Do you want to see my room?"

"Sure," I said.

"It was nice to meet you, Sweetie!" Ruth called after me.

"Nice to meet you too, Mrs. Fuller!" I called over my shoulder.

"Call me Ruth," she said.

Harrison and I disappeared into his room. His walls had many canvas paintings on each. They all said **H.F.** in the corner of them, where the artist normally writes his name. Then I noticed the easel, the paints, and brushes.

"You paint?" I asked.

Harrison nodded.

I examined the paintings. Each one was of a landscape or an abstract person. I discovered my favorite was one of a lighthouse on a rock island during a storm. The light in the lighthouse was off and a ship had crashed into the island.

"These are beautiful," I exclaimed.

Harrison shrugged like it was nothing.

"No really, they are awesome!" I repeated. "Have you ever sold any?"

"No, I haven't," Harrison replied. "The ones I don't keep, I normally donate to Goodwill. Surprisingly, they sell pretty quickly."

"Surprisingly?" I retorted. "Are you nuts? It would be surprising if they didn't sell. You should try selling some!"

"I'll think about it," he said, dismissively. "Anyway, let's get going."

The two of us made our way out of his bedroom and into the sitting room. It was empty.

We attempted to sneak out of the house, but Ruth came back into the room just as we opened the front door to leave. Luckily, her goodbye was short.

"Have a good time!" she said.

"Bye, Mom," Harrison said and led me to his car.

I climbed into the passenger seat.

While in the car, I pulled out my phone and pressed down on the top button. "Give me directions to the closest YMCA," I told it. Directions appeared on my phone, and I discovered that we were only about fifteen minutes away.

I showed Harrison the map before he started the engine, so he would know which street to head out on. He studied the map, and then we hit the road.

***

As soon as we got to the YMCA, I dashed into the changing room and changed out of my clothes and into my swimming suit.

By the time I got out to the pool, Harrison was waiting for me at the edge with his feet dangling in the water. I didn't waste another second—I jumped right into the water.

It felt cold at first, but soon I warmed up. I noticed Harrison still sitting on the edge.

"Come on get in!" I urged.

He pushed off the side and slid into the water.

He resurfaced and cried out, "Burr!"

Then he shook his head like a dog, spreading water from his hair. I put my hands up as a shield.

"You wanna' race?" I asked him.

He smiled his winning smile.

"Sure."

The pool was fairly crowded, so it took a while to decide where to race. We timed the start of our race so that just as this fat guy swam out of the way, we took off.

Olympic Bound

We both swam freestyle and turned into torpedoes jetting through the water.

Or, I was at least. Without looking I could tell Harrison was lagging. I hit the wall, pulled myself up on the edge, and sat with my legs in the pool.

When Harrison finally touched the wall, he looked up at me in wonder.

"How did you swim so fast?!" he asked.

I shrugged. "I don't know, I just can," I answered. "I have gotten faster since I starting practicing a week ago." I shrugged again.

"Well, however you're doing it, keep doing it," he said.

I beamed at that. It had been so long since someone had encouraged me to swim.

"Could you teach me how?" he asked.

I nodded. First, I instructed him to swim a lap so I could see what he was doing wrong. I stopped him halfway.

"No wonder I beat you so easily," I said. "It looks like you are slapping the water; you don't have your hands cupped right!" I showed him the proper way, but he couldn't quite master the first part—not slapping the water.

After a half-hour, he finally gave up. "Thanks for the lesson, but can we just swim for fun now?" he asked.

"Sure." I replied.

***

After another half-hour, we changed into our street clothes and went back to the car.

"Shoot!" I cried.

"What?"

"My hair!" I lamented. "It's wet! My mom will know I've been in the water. I didn't even think about that!" I scanned my brain for believable excuses, but none came to mind.

"We could drive around with the windows down until your hair dries," he suggested. I guessed that would have to work.

So that was what we did for the next half-hour. We drove and drove and drove. At least I got to see more of Florida, even if it was mostly too dark to see anything, except for what was illuminated by streetlights and the car lights.

I also learned more about Harrison. "So what do you want to be career wise?" I asked him.

Olympic Bound

He bit his lip, before admitting, "I know it's stupid, and unlikely, but I want to be an artist."

"Why is that stupid and unlikely?" I asked. "Like I said earlier, you are great at painting."

Without answering, Harrison asked me the same question that I had initially posed to him.

"Now, my dream is stupid and unlikely," I mimicked. "I want to be an Olympic swimmer. But how is that ever going to happen if I can't even practice swimming without doing it secretly?"

"What are the requirements for becoming an Olympic swimmer?" Harrison asked.

"There are a lot of steps, but the big one is you have to get first or second at the USA Swimming Olympic Trials Swim Meet," I explained. "If you get third or fourth, you may get to be a relay swimmer, but that is only if they don't already have enough people on the team."

He nodded as if he understood just how hard it was to want to be something that may be too far out of your reach to accomplish.

We were silent for a few moments before Harrison spoke again.

"Your hair looks about dry," he said. "Do you want to go home, now?"

I shrugged. I really didn't want to go home. I wished I could drive around with Harrison all night, but I finally decided it was probably time to go. I didn't want to break my curfew.

I got home and spotted police officers out front of my condo. I gasped. If anything had happened to Mom, I'm not sure I could live with myself.

Chapter 19 - Unbelievable

I burst through the door, ran up the stairs with Harrison tagging along behind me. I struggled through the heavy door at the top of the stairs, before getting inside, where I spotted Mom standing and talking with an officer. I let out a sigh of relief. She wasn't hurt — at least not that I could tell.

"Mom! What happened?!" I asked her.

She was startled at first, because she didn't realize I had come in, but she quickly recovered.

"Taylor, there was a break-in while I was out buying groceries," she said. "A few things were taken, but the police are working to find the culprit."

I shook my head with disbelief. We have had more bad luck than anyone I could think of! Why would we be vandalized? It was obvious we didn't have much. Why would anyone steal from the poor?

"I was about to text you, so you wouldn't worry when you got home and saw all the police," Mom said apologetically.

First, Dad died. Then, Mel died. Now, someone broke into our house? Unbelievable!

"We just can't catch a break, can we?" I asked her.

She shook her head, mournfully.

"So what was taken?" I questioned. She shrugged.

"Well, the TV, the radio, my empty purses, my laptop, my charger, my phone charger, maybe your phone charger—I'm not sure—a lamp, my grandmother's antique necklace, and my cheap fashion jewelry."

I nodded. Those things are about what I expected to be stolen, since they were the only things of any value that we owned.

"How did they get in?" I had noticed the door didn't look like it had been kicked in, and I didn't see any windows broken.

"We think they broke in via the window," she said.

I searched around the place again, seeing neither a broken window nor any shattered glass.

"Supposedly, a van that said 'Charles Roofing' was parked out front, and the employees got up on the roof, and then came in through an unlocked window. But there is no Charles Roofing Business here in Florida," she clarified.

"And how did you find that out?" I asked.

"A neighbor saw it, but didn't call the police until they started bringing items out through the front door," she answered.

I wondered how thick a person could be! How would burglars not get caught—even with a roofing cover-up—if they started bring TVs and radios through the front door and loading them into their van? Morons.

"So, you'll catch them, right?" I asked the officer. He gazed at me with an unreadable expression.

"We hope so," he replied. "Given all the info we have already uncovered, it is likely you will have your valuables back by tomorrow. I'm not making any promises, though."

I nodded in understanding.

Then, I remembered Harrison, who was still standing behind me. I turned around to face him.

"I'll see you in school tomorrow," I said.

He nodded. "Guess I'll go now," he said. "And hey, I hope the cops get your stuff returned."

He awkwardly hugged me before going back down the stairs and out the door.

***

In the morning, I woke up around 6:00 A.M. and decided to watch the video of the accident on www.crazydisastersinflorida.com, just to see Mel again. Seeing her body limp on the ground was almost too much to bear, and I wondered why I was putting myself through this torture all over again.

Then, I noticed there was a new entry on the site. I scanned through it.

Just Their Luck

Not long after the tragic crash that led to Melody Reeve's death, Taylor Reeve and her mother were robbed by a group of men claiming to be roof repairmen.

The group was first spotted by Mrs. Beeswax, a neighbor of Taylor and her mother. The "roof repairmen" climbed in through an unlocked window and stole valuable items, including jewelry and electronic devices, before escaping out the front door.

When suspicious Mrs. Beeswax saw the men carrying a TV, radio, etcetera, she decided to call the police. The police arrived only moments after the men left.

Taylor's mother was surprised to come home to a group of police officers standing in front of her condo. Taylor was just as surprised when she came home hours later.

The police are still searching for the men responsible for the robbery.

Keep checking this site to hear more about Taylor's bad luck!

I closed my computer and sat there in disbelief. It made sense how they found out about the crash, but how did they find this out? It wasn't like I had told anyone.

Were they watching the house or something? I hated to think that could be the case. It seemed creepy that, right now, there might be someone sitting in a car with a donut in one hand and a pad of paper in the other, keeping tabs on my life. It was too creepy a thought to entertain, so I quickly dismissed it.

I got up and stepped into the shower. Showers weren't anything like swimming, but it would have to do for now. After the shower, I made my way out to the kitchen. Mom was making hash browns and biscuits.

Not exactly the healthiest breakfast, but at least it would taste good.

"You're up early," I said to her.

"So are you," she replied. "When I heard the shower running, I decided to start breakfast." I sat down at the table and watched her work from behind.

"Mom, I love you," I said, after a moment. I was only just beginning to realize that I don't say it enough. Mom turned her head away from the potatoes.

"I love you too, Honey," she told me, before going back to cooking.

"So how has work been?" I asked her.

"Boring, like most jobs. How is school?" she asked.

"Boring, like most schools," I replied.

"No doubt," she said. She placed the spatula down and sat across from me at the table.

"Honey, are you, ok?" she asked me. I don't know what triggered her to say that. Maybe I was sighing too much, or making a weird face, or maybe she was just asking me because she was wondering if I was ok, after everything that had been happening over the past few weeks.

Olympic Bound

"No, I'm not ok, but how could I be after all this?" I answered.

"I know," she replied. "That is why I think it is time for you to start swimming again. You used to be so happy in the water. That is why I am going to let you start going back to the pool. We can go and pick up a swimsuit after school," she announced.

I gasped! Really? Just like that? She was going to let me swim?

KD Lee Writes

Chapter 11 – Picking Up

Wait. Mom... was... going... to... buy... me... a... swimsuit!

I still couldn't wrap my head around it. I didn't have to fake being excited; now I didn't have to lie to her about going to the pool.

"Really? Oh, my gosh! Thanks!" I told her, hugging her around the waist. She stoked my hair with the back of her hand.

"Just don't get hurt, ok?" she told me.

I nodded.

"I won't," I promised. She let go of me, and I was left to wonder what had changed her mind.

"And don't swim in the ocean, just the pool."

At the risk of her changing her mind, I bravely asked her why she had decided to let me swim again.

"My counselor convinced me," Mom said. "I had told him about how you were acting so out of sorts, and I couldn't get you out of your funk. He asked if there was anything that made you happy. Whatever that thing was, he said you should do more of it. It took me several sessions with him to finally admit that I had stopped letting you swim, when—well, you know. I knew it was wrong, and I hope you can forgive me."

I was stunned. The only thing I could say was, "Oh Mom!" I wrapped my arms around her even tighter.

"I hope letting you swim helps bring your old self back," Mom said after a moment.

Inside, not only did I feel a spark of life, but I felt more determined than ever to make it to the Olympics. Not only just for me, but for Dad and Mel.

***

I crawled up into the bus and sat down next to Jasmine. She had actually had saved me a seat.

First period was slow and boring. I sat in the back, so I could catch up on some math homework. The teacher was so absorbed in teaching us about World War I that she didn't even notice that I was doing other work until about halfway through her lesson.

Olympic Bound

"Taylor," Mrs. Baker said, "I understand that you have endured a terrible loss, but I would still appreciate it if you paid attention."

"I was paying attention Mrs. Baker," I replied, caustically.

"Then surly you can tell me when World War I started and when it ended?"

"Yes Ma'am." I scanned my brain for the answer.

"It started July 28, 1914 and ended November 11, 1918. In Europe, November 11 is known as Armistice Day and Remembrance Day. Here, it's the day we commemorate war veterans." Mrs. Baker gaped at me through squinted eye lids.

"That is correct, Miss Reeve," she said before plunging back into her lecture.

I turned back to my math, proud of myself for coming up with the correct answer. It wasn't like she asked a difficult question; she was probably going easy on me because of Mel.

The next class was just a video against hazing, and they put the juniors and sophomores together since there were fewer juniors and sophomores than seniors and freshman. That meant that I was in the same class as Harrison for once.

KD Lee Writes

Harrison, who sat right in front of me, faked stretched his arms out and dropped a note on my desk. I opened it furtively, making sure that Mr. Green didn't notice.

I read the note quickly:

I had a fun time yesterday. Maybe we can do it again sometime? How about Friday night?

-H

I tore a strip of paper from my notebook and thought about what to write back. I really wanted to just lie in bed all weekend and feel sorry for myself... or swim.

Do you feel like swimming again? If not that's cool we can do something else. Maybe a movie?

-T

I handed it to him while Mrs. Baker was facing the white board. Harrison read my note and then turned the paper around. He scribbled something down on the back of it before passing it to me again.

Swimming sounds great! Maybe I'll finally get good enough to beat you in a race! But that's unlikely. So, Friday at 6?

-H

Olympic Bound

I quickly scribbled a reply:

See you then. ☺

-T

I passed the final note to Harrison and turned my attention back to the video.

At free period, I found Jasmine. She was sitting in the grass, talking with Kate.

"Hey guys, where is Taffeta and the others?" I asked.

"Taffeta is so stuck up," Jasmine said. "We decided to become the three musketeers!"

"Who's the third?" I asked.

"You, of course!" Kate said. "So, what are you doing this weekend? Jasmine is sleeping over at my house, you want to come?"

I thought about her offer for a moment. I would rather be swimming all weekend now that Mom would let me. But I guessed I could swim up until it was time to go to the sleepover. On second thought, no. I wanted to spend as much time swimming as I could.

"I'm a little busy," I told them.

"No prob, maybe another time," Kate suggested.

***

After school, I took my time getting home, so I could tell Mom that I had bought a swimsuit on the way home. I wouldn't want her to waste money buying me another suit I don't need.

I slipped it on and made my way down to the pool. Mom tagged along, probably to make sure I didn't drown my "first" time back in the pool. Of course it wasn't my first time back in the pool—it was my first time back with her supervising—but she didn't know that.

I dove into the pool without any hesitation. My sudden movements about gave my mom a heart attack.

"Taylor! Don't dive! It is too shallow!" She tried to tell me when I surfaced. I rolled my eyes.

"Look at the sign! It clearly says no diving!" She said, as she pointed to a sign hanging from a nail pounded into the side of the pool house.

"Mom, it is ten feet deep," I said. "That is plenty deep for diving."

"How about you just swim some laps on your first time back out?" she suggested.

"Fine," I replied. I did about fifty laps before Mom got my attention and beckoned me to come over to the side of the pool. I swam over and she crouched down to talk to me.

"What?" I asked.

"I am going to trust you to be safe, ok?" she said. "I'm going up to the house to do some work."

"Ok, bye," I said dismissively.

She looked like she was about to change her mind, but didn't and left through the fence surrounding the pool.

-One Hundred and Fifty Laps Later-

I walked through the door of my house and found Mom sitting at the table reading something on her computer.

"Mom?" I asked.

"Yes, Sweetie?" she replied.

"I was thinking," I began, "could I ask the swim coach if it was alright that I practiced with them?"

"But hasn't season already started?" she asked.

"Yes . . . but maybe I could still practice with them, just not compete?" I said, hedging.

She sighed, heavily. "Why don't we just take things one step at a time?" she said.

***

After school the next day, I stopped by the high school's swimming pool. *Yeah, they have their own swimming pool!* I walked up to the coach.

"May I help you?" he inquired.

"I was wondering if I could practice with your team," I began. "I'm aware that the season has already started, but I was hoping I could just practice with you and then join the team next year?"

"I don't see anything wrong with that," the coach replied. "Sessions are every day after school from 3-5. We are a little short on swimmers anyway."

"Is that it, then?" I asked. "Or do I have to fill out some papers?"

"That's it," he said. "And sorry, but what is your name, again? I've seen you in school before, but you aren't in my classes..."

"Taylor, Taylor Reeve," I said.

"Pleasure to meet you, Taylor," he said and extended his hand for me to shake. "I'm Coach Hamton. Welcome to the team."

Olympic Bound

Junior Year

KD Lee Writes

Olympic Bound

CHAPTER 12 – ONE MEDAL DOWN

"Go! Taylor! WOO-HOO!" I heard Mom, Harrison, Jasmine, and Kate shout from the stands. I hoped I was in the lead, but I couldn't tell. I was too focused on swimming as hard and as fast as I could.

I was closing in on the cement wall; finally, it was close enough for me to do my turnaround. I did a little flip in the water and turned myself, pushing off the wall as hard as I could with my feet. I kept both of my arms out and jetted through the water.

I resurfaced and resumed my freestyle stroke all the way to the other end. Another flip-turn! I jetted through the water again, with my hands out front. I just had to get back down to the other end now.

I hit the wall and pulled myself out. I looked to my right and squinted so I could see the leaderboard. I was first!

KD Lee Writes

I won! Two more girls pulled themselves out of the water.

Once every girl was out of the water, including the straggler, I got to claim my medal. Mom took a picture of me with the second and third place winners.

"Good job, Honey!" Mom said. Harrison hugged me, and then I quickly ran to the locker room to change into some dry clothes. After that, we all headed out to the car so we could celebrate at our favorite restaurant.

I wore the medal around my neck until we got to the restaurant. Harrison opened my door for me, and I climbed out. The restaurant was my favorite Chinese place in town.

Mom beat Harrison to the restaurant door and opened it for all of us. The interior was decorated with Chinese lanterns, paintings and pictures of China, a little dragon fountain, and a Buddha statue. Each booth and table had Chinese symbols carved into them.

A guy in his early thirties showed us to a table, and the five of us sat down.

"You were amazing, Taylor!" Kate said, once we were settled with our menus.

"Thanks," I said modestly.

"No, you were supercalifragilisticexpialidocious!" Jasmine said.

Olympic Bound

"Isn't that from Mary Poppins?" I asked.

"Yeah, but it is a real word—I looked it up," she said. "It means, super, super, amazingly, awesome!"

"Thanks," I replied. I felt myself blush.

"Hey, why didn't you wear your medal into the restaurant?" Jasmine asked.

"I decided to leave it in the car," I replied with a shrug.

After the waitress took our drink orders, Mom turned to me and asked, "Taylor, would you like to share some more good news with your friends?"

I smiled and said, "I am going to the USA Swimming Olympic Trials Qualifications!"

KD Lee Writes

Olympic Bound

CHAPTER 13 - STATIC

Harrison, who had gotten really good at swimming, since we started dating around the Winter Dance last year, agreed to train with me after swimming practice each day. I needed to be ready for the USA Swimming Olympics Trial Qualifications.

In order to participate in the Trials, I had to be a USA Swimming Member. To qualify, I had to swim in an event down here in Florida; my time was good enough to allow me to advance. I also had to fill out a form online. But other than that, my focus had been on practice.

I tried to think positively. I knew I had as much a chance of making it to the USA Swimming Olympics Trials, and then to the Olympics, as anyone else that was good enough to qualify. I could have waited another four years, but I wanted the challenge now.

I planned on qualifying for all the freestyle races, two breaststroke races, and the two medley races. This meant that I had to practice every stroke. The medley competitions were divided into fourths. The first fourth was the butterfly stoke, then the back stroke, followed by the breaststroke, and finally—my favorite—the freestyle stroke.

Butterfly was my second favorite. I loved flying out of the water like that, but it also was the one that tired me out the most.

***

For our practices, Harrison and I drove to the YMCA for both the bigger pool, and so he could time me. On the 50-meter freestyle, I was supposed to finish in 26.19 or less. The stopwatch on Harrison's phone consistently told me that I still needed to shave off one second from my time. I hoped that by the time of the qualifying competition, I would have shaved off three seconds; I wanted the extra cushion.

On the 100-meter freestyle, I needed to clock in no slower than 56.49 seconds. Even with that one—my best stroke—I still had one and a half seconds to shave off.

After a half-hour of me swimming and Harrison timing, he finally asked if he could get in.

Olympic Bound

"What?" I asked, "Of course, sorry, I didn't mean to get you stuck on timer duty."

"It's all good," he said, jumping in.

The YMCA was pretty quiet right now. If it wasn't, he wouldn't have done that.

"So, how long have you been keeping Qualifications a secret?" he asked.

"About two weeks," I said "But isn't it exiting!? If I qualify, I get to go to the Trials, and then to the Olympics!"

Harrison smiled at me. "I hope everything works out," he said and then kissed me tenderly on the lips. Even though we have been dating for over a year, I still get butterflies every time he does that.

"Race you, two laps," he said.

"You're going down!" I replied.

I broke into a freestyle stroke and we raced to the end of the pool. When we finish the race, or when I finished the race anyway, I looked back.

Harrison was just finally catching up. He still had not won a race against me. *I think it got to him a little bit, but he never said anything.* He could still beat me at mini-golf anytime he wanted.

KD Lee Writes

***

The whole week I worked at getting faster. I even started weight lifting to get stronger.

Coach Hamton almost shot through the roof, with happiness, when I told him about Qualifications on Monday. Now, he was pushing me extra hard in practice. He took it upon himself to time me as well.

On Tuesday, I was surprised to find all the girls standing around in a huddle on the outside of the pool when I got to swim practice ten minutes late.

"What are you girls doing out of the pool?" I asked.

"Take a look," Samantha grimaced.

I peeked past them, and I saw that the pool water was red. My first thought was blood, but then there would be cops all over the place. No, this has to be a prank. The graffiti on the wall was proof:

Coach Hamton You Stink!

Great. Now how were we supposed to practice? I spotted the principal and coach talking over by the short diving board. I made my way past the little group of gossiping swim-team girls and over to them.

"Coach! Who did this?" I asked.

He turned at the sound of my voice.

"Ah, Taylor, there you are!" Coach Hamton said.

"Coach, what happened? Who did this?" I asked.

"We don't know," he replied. "Sadly, there are no cameras installed around the pool."

"We're going to have to drain the pool and replace it with new water," the principal said sadly.

"How long until the pool will be reopened?" I asked.

"I'd say about two weeks," he replied. "All the pool guys are booked up until next week."

I sighed.

"Are you going to be able to figure out who did this?" I asked.

"Probably not without camera footage of the culprits," he said.

"So is practice cancelled?" I asked.

"It is today," he replied. "We're looking into maybe moving practice somewhere else, but no one wants a group of teenage girls taking up pool space. Your moms will receive emails keeping you updated."

I nodded.

"So, should I go home then?" I asked.

"Wait a second," Coach Hamton said. "I wanted to talk to you about something before you leave."

The principal walked over to tell the girls to go home.

"Yeah?" I said to Coach Hamton.

He spent a few minutes talking to me about exercises to make me stronger for Qualifications.

"Thanks Coach, see you, uh, soon I hope," I said.

I made my way out of the building and to my car. Mom gave it to me for my seventeenth birthday! It was awesome, not because it was some expensive Ferrari or anything; just being a car made it awesome!

Being a Chevy Ultra, it was a lot like Harrison's car, actually. I cranked up the radio and sang along with it as I drove home.

Mom wasn't home, yet, when I arrived, so I pulled on a swimsuit and headed down to the pool.

It was fairly crowded because of the warm sunny weather. It was way too crowded to swim laps. I headed back to the house and changed, so I could bike ride instead. Coach had said it would strengthen my leg muscles and help me kick faster.

I hauled my bike from the bike rack and took off for the park. It was about a mile down the road from the condo.

You could barely call it a park, although it did have a mini playground. Mostly it was just a bunch of gravel and dirt trails through some woods. The woods down in Florida were a lot different from the ones in Indiana. The types of trees around were mostly palm trees, pine trees, and a few other varieties. The nature was not nearly as diverse as it was in Indiana. Moss also hung down from many of the branches.

Once I was on the bike trail at the park, I turned a corner only to see a snake sprawled across the trail. Normally, I would have hit the brakes, but I was too close to the snake to stop in time; if I hit the brakes, I would probably fly off and onto the snake. Instead, I swerved quickly, but I unfortunately ran over its tail. I was sure it would be fine though.

There were other animals along the trail, too, like birds, squirrels, and lizards. Florida was crawling with them. I looked them up; the lizards you find everywhere were anoles. I saw the little critters constantly. Farther down the trail, I spotted a sign unlike the other ones:

Alligator Crossing

Behind it was a tiny lake connected to two canals. I got closer to the lake and discovered another sign.

Do not feed the alligators!

(500 Dollar Fine & Up to 60 days in Jail)

I parked my bike by the sign and stared into the lake. In the middle of it, I caught two eyes staring back at me. Alligator eyes! I watched the gator floating there, continuing to watch me. It started swimming closer, but there were still twenty yards of water and fifteen yards of land between us. I wasn't scared, yet. I stood my ground and watched it some more. I only decided to return to my bike when it was five yards from the land.

I headed back to my bike and continued down the trail. The temperature was about 90 degrees, with just as much humidity, and I was sweating profusely. I would have loved a bottle of water just then. But I kept pressing on. I needed to train hard and under extreme conditions, if I wanted to be prepared for Qualifications.

When I reached a dead end, I made up my mind to go home. Since moving down to Florida, I had gotten used to 80-degree weather, but I still struggled when it climbed up into the 90s.

When I reached a clearing further down the trail, I gasped. There, right in front of me, was a half-ton, eleven-foot-long alligator sprawled across my trail, sunbathing.

I stared at him, petrified. I took one foot off my bike pedal and planted it on the ground to keep me from falling over. I knew little about alligators, except how to tell them apart from crocodiles. *Alligators have sharp*

Olympic Bound

teeth that can kill you in one bite, and they are faster on land than you would expect.

I stood there for what seemed like forever, locked in the most intense staring contest of all time. But then, again, this was Florida for you. I started walking backwards, slowly rolling my bike with me, so I wouldn't provoke the gator.

The left pedal hit my shin, and I stumbled backward, letting out a shout of pain as the pedal cut into my leg. I fell over, and the bike followed, landing on top of me. I got up as quickly as possible, not liking to be so vulnerable. I looked at the alligator. It sat unmoving. I let out a sigh of relief that it hadn't come after me, and I turned my bike around. I got up on it and pedaled back towards the trail's dead end. Not knowing what else to do, I called Mom.

"Hey, Sweetie!" She answered. "What's wrong? Are you, ok?"

"Sort of," I said. "I rode my bike to the park. But on my way back I discovered an alligator across the trail. I can't go around it because there is water, alligator infested water, on both sides."

I heard the panic in Mom's voice as she suggested, "Stay calm and don't get close to it. Maybe just wait until it moves?"

"Mom I..." I heard static from the other end.

"Mom, are you there?"

-Static-

"Mom?" I looked down at my phone.

CALL ENDED

I stuffed my phone back in my pocket and stood there with my bike, regretting my bike-ride idea. I spotted a dark cloud in the distance through the trees. It looked totally out of place in the picture-perfect sky. *Wouldn't it just make this day so great if it started to rain?*

Half-an-hour had passed since I had to stop because of the alligator blocking my path, and things hadn't gotten any better. In fact, this day had gotten worse and worse as it progressed. Now, rain drizzled down from a dark cloud hanging over me. I could see blue sky in the distance, but there was one dark cloud hanging over me, just like you see in cartoons.

There wasn't any lightening, and the rain was only at a trickle, so at least there was something to be grateful for. I rode back up to the clearing every once in a while to check on the alligator, and to see if I could get by it yet. Nope. It was still motionless.

I tried my cell again, too, but it wouldn't even make a phone call now that the battery was so dead. Great.

I seemed to have the worst of luck. Of course, the alligator had chosen to stretch out on the trail once I had ridden past it to a dead-end. Of course, the "roofers" from last year had to pick our condo to rob. (We never did get that stuff back, but insurance covered the electronics). Of course, that trucker chose our car to pull out in front of the one time I let Mel sit in the front seat. Of course, that riptide occurred while my dad was swimming. Of course, of course, of course!

I broke out in frustrated tears. It started to rain harder. I was so tired of all this bad luck. I was just sick of it! I yelled into the rain in an attempt to make myself feel better.

"I HATE MY BAD LUCK!" I screamed as loud as I could. Surprisingly, it made me feel better even though it didn't help my situation any.

I rode back up to the clearing and decided to stay put and watch the alligator from the woods. If it decided it was hungry, I could take off on my bike. The only problem was that the dirt trail had turned to brown, gooey mud—not the best terrain for biking. It was getting worse by the second, too, so I hoped the alligator would move soon. I wanted to escape this situation, before it got too bad.

"Please move," I begged.

"Move, please," I whispered again, more for my own benefit than for his.

While I stood there waiting, I thought up a name for the alligator; there wasn't much else that I could do while I waited for it to slip off the trail. I picked a name that could be a girl's name or a boy's name: Mason.

"Mason, go into the lake," I instructed sternly, feeling a little foolish talking to an alligator.

It didn't move; it just remained sprawled out there.

Maybe if I made a lot of noise, it would creep into the water.

I got my bike ready for a quick escape and started screaming as loudly as I could.

Still, the alligator didn't move. I stopped screaming. After about five minutes of silence, though, it finally got up. My eyes widened, and I didn't move. Ignoring me, it sauntered slowly into the water, disappearing beneath the surface.

"Yes!" I exclaimed.

I immediately got on my bike and rode down the path. I was pummeled by rain as I entered the clearing.

It seemed like an eternity while I made my way into the woods again and followed the many signs back to the parking lot. Before long, I was back at home and inside, warming up under the covers of my bed.

Olympic Bound

I still had a little over an hour until I had to meet Harrison at the YMCA to practice swimming. Normally, I swam for three hours every day, but today I would probably only get one, just because of some punk vandalizing the pool. Poor Coach, what an awful thing to have had written about him on the wall.

I debated whether I should call Harrison to meet me early at the Y, so I would get at least two hours, but I decided against it and took a nap instead. I was exhausted, and I would swim faster well rested anyway.

KD Lee Writes

Chapter 14 – Birthday Planner

I met Harrison at the pool after a good nap. He was already sitting with his feet in the water when I arrived.

"Hey," he said, getting up and kissing me.

"Practice was canceled today," I told him when we broke apart.

"What! Why?" he asked.

"Someone dyed the pool red and wrote graffiti on the wall, so it has been cancelled for about two weeks," I said.

Harrison sighed, knowing what this meant to me. Qualifications were only a month and a half away, so cancelled practice meant I wasn't being coached anymore—well, at least until practice started up again.

"Are you going to be coming here more often?" he questioned.

"I guess, since it has been raining recently, I'll have to practice indoors," I replied.

Harrison nodded solemnly.

"I'll practice with you the whole three hours if you want," he said.

I smiled, thinking how good he was to me, but I couldn't ask him to do that. It wouldn't be fair to him.

"Nah, that's ok," I said. "How about you just keep meeting me at our regular practice time." I added.

"You sure?" he asked.

"Positive," I replied.

***

After my last class (geometry with Mr. Dame), I made my way out to Harrison's car. Now that I didn't have swimming practice, he was driving me to and from school. We arrived at the car right at the same time.

"I know you need to go to practice swimming, but I have a big favor to ask you," Harrison said.

"Yeah?" I replied.

"It's my sister's birthday on Sunday, but I was thinking about having a surprise party for her on Saturday," he said. "Would you be up for helping me plan it?"

Amy, his younger sister, was the cutest, sweetest, and smartest little girl. Of course I would help! Oh, and how sweet was Harrison for planning a surprise party for her!?

"Of course!" I said. "How old will she be? Seven?"

"Yeah, seven, and she loves Barbie, so I was thinking that could be the theme, but I know nothing about that stuff, so that is where you come in," he said.

"You think that just because I'm a girl, I know about Barbie?" I asked. "I've never even owned one! But yeah, I can help with that. Mel, she had a few." I fought to keep my emotions at bay.

Luckily, after a year of practice, I was better able to control them. Harrison got awkward for a moment with the mention of my sister, but he got over it pretty quickly.

"I can practice a little later today if you want to get started," I suggested.

"Ok, boss," he said. "What is step one?"

"Maybe we should make a list of things we need, people to invite, and where is it going to be? Will it be at your house?" I asked.

"I was thinking so, but she really likes this place called Sky Zone," he said. "It is a huge trampoline park, and they have birthday rooms that you can rent, but I don't know how much that would cost."

"What is your budget?" I asked.

"Mom gave me a hundred and fifty dollars to spend," he replied.

"That's it?" I asked. "In that case, Sky Zone probably won't work out once you factor in the cost of things like food, cake, decorations, and a party room rental, but we can look into it." Feeling in the mood to start immediately, I added, "Turn around. Let's go to Walmart first and pick out some decorations."

Harrison did a U-turn, and we headed back to the Walmart that we had just passed.

"What exactly are we getting?" he asked.

"Anything that has to do with birthday parties and Barbie's," I answered. I pulled a piece of paper out of my backpack and began making a list.

- Piñata
- Plastic Cups
- Plastic Plates
- Plastic Silverware
- Napkins
- Order a Barbie Cake

Olympic Bound

- Streamers
- Balloons
- Gift Bags
- Gift Presents (to put in gift bags)
- Various Barbie Decorations

I read the list out to Harrison, as we pulled into the Walmart parking lot.

"Sounds like you know what you're doing," he said, when I finished reading the list to him. I did have a lot of practice; I was practically a mom for a year. It felt good to something for a little sister again.

Once we were in the Walmart, Harrison chose a cart, and we walked to the party section.

There were more Barbie things than I expected. We even found Barbie cups, but no Barbie silverware or napkins. Instead, we chose the next best thing: pink silverware and napkins.

We decided to hold off on the cake since it was a little early to order it. Harrison went to work calling everyone to invite them to the party before it was too late, and they already had other plans. Thirty people had confirmed they were coming.

Five of them were Amy's friends, seven were parents, and the rest were family. Well, except for me. I was coming, but I didn't fit in any of those categories, so I wrote "1 party planner" on the list by my name. It was quicker than writing "1 birthday-girl's brother's girlfriend."

"Thanks for helping out," Harrison said, after our shopping was finished, and we were on the way to the pool.

"No problem," I replied. Just then, my phone rang, and I checked the caller ID—it was my mom.

"Hey, Mom," I answered. "What's up?"

"I got the tickets to fly out to Qualifications!" she said, excitedly.

***

It was the day of Amy's surprise birthday party, and I had convinced all my good friends to pitch in and help out.

"Thanks for coming over to help," I said to Kate, Jasmine, and Emily. Emily has been my friend since I got on the swimming team. She was just as excited for me as everyone else when I told her about Qualifications.

"No, problem," she said. "I just hope Amy likes it."

"Yeah, anytime," Kate said.

"I didn't have anything better to do anyway," Jasmine stated, sadly.

"Does one of you want to go and pick up the cake, while I put up the streamers?" I asked.

"I'll do it!" Emily offered.

"Ok, here is the receipt; you may have to show them that," I told her.

"Thanks, ok, see you gals in a few!" She took off out the door.

"Gals?" Jasmine asked, once Emily was gone. "Seriously?" Jasmine asked again.

Neither Jasmine nor Kate cared for Emily much. That was too bad; I thought she was sweet.

"Come on guys, be nice," I scolded them.

"Whatever," Jasmine said, putting up another pink streamer.

I pulled out a stool and weaved together a white streamer with her pink one.

"Are you and Harrison excited for prom?" Kate asked.

I bit my lip. In truth, we hadn't even talked about prom, but I assumed we were going together. Swimming was the only thing that had been on my mind recently.

"Uh, we haven't actually talked about it," I said.

"But you're going, right? I mean of course you are! You can't miss prom!" Jasmine exclaimed.

"I think so," I said. "Hey, would you guys like to go and help me pick out a dress?"

Both of them squealed.

"Of course!" they said in unison.

"JINX!" they cried at the same time. I rolled my eyes. They were such girlie-girls.

Next, I started putting the gift bags together. Kate helped. Each one was stuffed with one pink slinky, one pink silly putty, one mini Barbie notebook, one Barbie pen, one tootsie roll (Amy's favorite candy), and one uninflated, pink balloon.

Now there were a total of seven little girls coming to Amy's party, so I put together eight bags, adding in the extra, so that Amy could have one herself.

After filling the bags, I went into the kitchen to help Harrison's mom with the finger sandwiches.

"Hello, Taylor!" she said. "I just want to thank you again for helping out." I shrugged.

"No problem," I said.

"Harrison is so lucky to have you," Ruth said. "You are a very sweet girl."

"Thank you," I said awkwardly, and I pulled apart a slice of corned beef and stuck it on the mini sandwich, followed by some Munster cheese and lettuce. I heard the door slam. Harrison was back from the store—he had to make a last-minute supply run, because he had somehow forgotten to buy the party hats.

"Hey, Sweetie," I said, kissing him.

Harrison smiled at me and showed me the shopping bag.

"Got the party hats," he said, proudly.

I snatched them from him and set them in a stack next to the gift bags. Harrison got to work on the present table's tablecloth, while I went back to the kitchen.

When we were done making the sandwiches, I stuck a colored toothpick through each one on the serving tray and put the full tray in the refrigerator.

"Honey, go ahead and decorate," Ruth said to me. "I've got the food under control."

"Are you sure?" I asked.

"Positive," she said. "I got it."

I went back into the living room just as Emily was walking through the door, cake in hand.

"Hey y'all!" she said cheerfully. "This cake looks great!"

I took it from her and looked at it though the plastic window on the cardboard lid. It was lined with pink and had an icing landscape with two Barbies, in princess gowns, standing in the middle of the cake.

"Thanks Emily!" I said. "It does look great."

"Anytime," she said, with a wave of her hand.

I brought the cake into the kitchen and stuck it in the refrigerator by the mini sandwiches.

"It looks adorable!" Ruth exclaimed as she caught a peek of the cake.

"It does look pretty cute," I admitted, and I walked about out to help with the decorations.

Next, I hung the banner that announced how old Amy was. It read:

Happy 7th

Birthday!!!

Harrison helped tape it up, since I was a little too short to reach the ceiling, even with the aid of a step stool.

"Ta-da!" he said, jumping down from the tiny stool.

"What do you think?" he asked, tilting his head to the side to look at it from another angle.

I mimicked him.

"Looks good," I responded. "Alright, what else do we need to do? We have the table center pieces, the banner, the gift bags, the balloons, the cake, the snacks, which your mom is finishing up, the punch is in the refrigerator, the ice-cream is in the freezer, the streamers are up, the tablecloth is on the present table, and the party hats are out. Are we missing anything?"

"Sounds like we have it all," he said.

"No, there has to be something we're forgetting," I said, deep in thought. "Oh! The magic show! Did you call the magician and confirm?"

"I did," Harrison said. "He will be here a half-hour after the guests are supposed to arrive."

If you are wondering how we are paying for all this with just $150, we aren't. Harrison's mom dished out a bit more money when Harrison and I laid out our 7th Birthday Extravaganza Plan.

"Awesome!" I said. "OK, that's everything. Oh—and the presents we got her? Are they in your room? Let's put them on the table."

"Whatever you say, Boss!" he saluted me in a corny way and disappeared into his room.

Moments later, he emerged with one medium-sized party bag overflowing with colored paper and one wrapped-up box. He set the two of them down on the table.

"Now, are we ready?" he asked.

"Now, we just wait for the guests to arrive, and call your grandma when it is time for her to bring Amy over," I said. Amy was staying with her grandma until it was time for her party.

Suddenly, I remembered something. "I almost forgot!" I exclaimed. "Amy's birthday tiara! Where is it?"

"Um, not sure, but I will find it," Harrison said, and he dashed off to a pile of abandoned Walmart bags on the floor. Now, that everything was put up Emily, Jasmine, and Kate were all standing around talking about what shops they should raid for a prom dress.

"Are you guys staying for the party?" I asked.

"Nah, the three of us thought we'd go to the beach for a while. You're welcome to go with us, Taylor," Kate suggested.

Jasmine was rolling her eyes, probably annoyed they had to invite Emily to tag along.

"I think I am going to stay here and help Harrison and his mom serve ice cream and stuff," I said. "You guys have fun."

"Do you need anything else before we go?" Emily asked, sweetly.

Again, I couldn't understand why Kate and Jasmine hated her so much. She was so nice!

"Thanks, Emily, but I think Harrison and I have it covered," I said. "You guys haven't seen the tiara, though, have you?"

"Sorry, I don't think so," Emily said.

"It might be in the extra party bags? I'm not sure," Jasmine suggested.

"Hope you find it before Amy arrives!" Kate added.

The three girls went out to their parked cars in the driveway and headed to Fort Myers Beach. I didn't know what they were thinking, though—the beach at this time a day? The traffic would be horrific!

"Bye!" I called after them, waving.

Emily stuck her head out her car window.

"Call me sometime!" She said. "Maybe we can practice at the Y together before you fly off to Qualifications!"

"Ok, will do!" I called back.

Emily disappeared back inside her car and drove off to follow Jasmine and Kate, about the same time I reentered the house.

***

A little girl, around Amy's age or maybe a little bit younger, arrived with her mom five minutes early. They were the first two people to show up. Next, Harrison and Amy's aunts and uncles arrived, then additional guests, such as Amy and Harrison's older cousins.

Amy was set to arrive at any minute, so I went over the drill with everyone, aiming the rules more toward the little kids.

"So when we hear the doorbell, what do you do?" I asked the little girls.

"Hide!" They said, in unison.

"And what do you do when Amy and her grandma come inside?" I prompted them.

"Jump out and scream, 'Happy Birthday, Amy!'" They repeated.

"Ok, good job," I said.

Then the doorbell rang. All of us dove into our hiding places. The door opened. A second later Amy came inside.

All of us jumped out and shouted as loudly as we could muster, "Happy Birthday, Amy!"

She jumped back in surprise, and the ends of her mouth stretched up to her ears, in the biggest, widest smile.

"Thank you, guys!" she squealed, running up to hug her friends.

My smile stretched almost as wide as hers, just watching how happy she was.

"Happy Birthday, Amy," I said.

"Hi, Harrison's girlfriend!" she said, hugging me, too.

Harrison came up from behind me and held the crown above her head.

"I now pronounce Amy the princess of birthdays!" he said, setting the crown on her head. Somehow, her grin stretched impossibly wider.

She broke out in a fit of giggles and hugged him around the waist. I couldn't help but think of Mel when she was seven. Amy even looked a little like her.

KD Lee Writes

Olympic Bound

CHAPTER 15 – RANCE IT

A few days after the party, around the time I'd normally have team practice, Emily and I got together to swim.

"I don't think your friends like me much," Emily stated in a matter-of-fact tone.

"What gave you that vibe?" I asked.

"Well, you know when I went to the beach after helping you set up Amy's party?" she asked.

"Uh, yeah," I said, wondering what Kate and Jasmine had done that finally made Emily realize they didn't like her. She was normally so blind to that stuff; it must have been something bad. My face flushed with worry.

"Well, they asked me if I could run up and get them milkshakes at the DQ on the beach," she said. "Do you know where that is?" I nodded. It was literally ten yards from the pier.

"So I did," Emily continued. "Kate wanted vanilla and Jasmine wanted cherry. I didn't get anything for myself because I am trying to lose weight."

I stared her up and down. If anything, Emily could gain a few pounds. She looked like she was borderline anorexic.

"Well, when I got back, they were gone," Emily went on. "All their stuff was gone too, so I know they weren't like kidnapped or something, unless the kidnapper took all of their stuff, too. So I called them to ask where they were, but neither of them picked up. I had to throw away both milkshakes!" She said this like it was the most horrifying thing in the world.

"Thank goodness you drove separately!" I said, aghast.

"Luckily!" she agreed, exasperated.

"I'm so sorry they did that to you," I admitted. "They can be a bit bitchy sometimes."

She shrugged to tell me that it wasn't my fault. Then, out of nowhere, she took off swimming. Other than me, Emily was the fastest on the team. She was skinny, but lengthy and fast. The girls on the team have been calling her "Teeny Torpedo" recently. She took it as a complement, but I don't think that was what the girls had in mind.

I started swimming after her. After a few laps, she fell behind, but was still right on my tail. I pulled ahead ever further, and, after my fifth lap, I was ahead of her by a full lap. We took a break at fifty laps to soak and chat for a bit.

"So how did the party go?" Emily asked me.

"Good, except one of the girls stuck a piece of a pretzel stick up her nose and it took her mom ten minutes to fish it out with a pair of Harrison's mom's tweezers," I said.

Emily showed sympathy instead of laughing like Jasmine would have.

"How dreadful!" Emily said. "Was she ok?"

I shrugged. Dreadful? Emily really did have a strange way of saying things.

"She cried a lot, but I don't think she was really hurt," I assured her.

"So what are you doing after swimming?" Emily asked. "Want to catch a bite to eat?"

"Sorry, Emily, I would love to, but Harrison and I are going out." I said. "He says he has something to ask me."

"No biggie," she responded. "Alright, let's get back to swimming, future medalist."

I smiled and dove back in.

***

"Hey Harrison," I said, wrapping my arms around him to kiss him. "So what do you need to ask me?"

"Would you, Taylor Nicole Reeve, accompany me to the senior prom?" he asked.

"Of course!" I accepted. "But only so I can see you in a tux. You are renting one?"

"I guess so," he replied. "Do you have your dress already?"

"I'm going shopping with Jasmine and Kate soon, but no, not yet," I replied.

The two of us sat down in the booth at our favorite spot—Bahama Breeze. It has great meals, but you can't beat their yucca fries, even though the first word sounds like yuck-a. At least that is how I say it. I've heard others pronounce it you-ca, so I am not exactly sure how you are supposed to pronounce it.

"You're getting the yucca fries, I assume?" Harrison asked.

I nodded. Unlike me, Harrison disliked them. I didn't get why. They were almost like square-ish potato fries. Potatoes and yucca were very similar.

"And the wood-grilled chicken with broccoli and sweet potatoes?" He asked.

I am so predictable.

"Yes," I replied. "And you are getting a cheeseburger with lettuce and tomatoes?"

"Always," he said.

Guess it wasn't just me that was predictable.

"Actually no," Harrison amended. "I am going to be a rebel and add onions."

***

After lunch, I drove home and called Emily, deciding I would rather go shopping with her than with Jasmine and Kate.

"Hey Emily," I said. "Do you already have a prom dress?"

"Um, I'm not going to prom," she said.

"What?! No one asked you?" I asked.

"No, a few guys asked me, but I don't think I am going," she said.

"Why?" I inquired.

"I just don't really want to," she said. I shook my head. That wasn't a very good reason.

"But you have to go," I said. "I mean; it *is* prom after all! This is your last chance to go!" Like me, Emily was a senior, so it really was her last chance.

"I don't really like dancing," she said.

I thought this over.

"You don't like to? Or you can't?" I asked.

"Maybe more the second one," she admitted.

"I can teach you," I offered. "When I was thirteen, I took dance lessons for a year. Then we can pick out dresses together!"

I heard her sigh into the phone.

"How about I teach you some dance moves after swimming practice at the Y every day leading up to prom?" I said.

"But don't you go out with Harrison then?" Emily asked.

"Normally, but he'll understand," I said. "If you don't want to, I won't push it anymore, but come on! It's prom!"

"Ok, if you really think you can teach me," Emily said.

"I know I can," I replied.

Chapter 16 – Spare the Toes

Emily's first dance lesson had already been in session for over an hour now, and it wasn't going well. Harrison came over to help out. He was a fairly good dancer, himself.

"Maybe try it with Harrison for a while," I said, sinking into a chair, clutching my toes. Emily had just stepped on them with her high heels. I had on open-toe heels, so that hadn't helped.

"You sure you don't mind?" Emily asked. "I mean; he is your boyfriend."

"Seriously? You're just dancing!" I said. "Anyway, maybe it will help to try with a new partner?" Mostly, I just wanted to give my toes a moment to heal from being stomped on.

I restarted the mix CD we'd been dancing along to. I'd filled it with songs you might hear at prom—fast ones and slow ones. Emily started right in, but she fell (on accident, not as a dance move) into Harrison. He caught her before she could hit the ground.

"Maybe you should wear flat foot shoes," I offered. "It could be you just aren't very balanced in heels." Emily shook her head.

"I suck no matter how you look at it, but I can try," she said and took off her shoes. She set them to the side.

I restarted the music and noticed that she was doing a lot better barefoot.

Harrison gave her a few tips, but nothing new. Basically, she just needed to loosen up. She looked like a clumsy robot. I knew that was harsh, but it was true.

"I told you guys!" she exclaimed. "I can't dance! I'm like a fish out of water here!" Emily pushed back from Harrison and went to sit in one of the chairs we had scooted back to make room for dancing.

"Emily, you just need to work on it a little," I said. "You aren't that bad. Here, let's try something," I pulled her to her feet and dragged her to the middle of the "dance floor".

"Stand on one leg as long as you can," I said.

"Why?" she asked.

"Just, do it," I ordered. Emily sighed and lifted up a leg, balancing on her right foot.

"Now do that as long as you can," I said.

Before long, she started to lean forward and put her left foot down to steady herself before she fell.

"I counted," I said. "That was fifteen seconds. With dancing, you have to be well balanced. If you can stand on one leg for over a minute you will be able to balance better when you dance, even in heels."

Instead of contesting, she lifted up her right leg this time and balanced for a maybe a few seconds longer.

"There," I said. "You got it. But since the dance is only in another week, we might want to get back to dancing, and you can practice the balance trick at home."

My dance teacher, when I was younger, had made a poor, little, shy girl, who was really clumsy, do this trick for half the dance class every session, so she would achieve better balance. She quit taking classes a week later. Likely from the embarrassment of having to do it while all the other girls could see her while they practiced their dance routines.

I hoped the results with Emily were better. It wasn't like I was mocking her in front of a whole class like my instructor had done to that girl. This was different.

"I think I just shouldn't go," Emily said. "I don't even have a date to prom, and like you said, it is only a week away."

"What about the boys who asked you?" I queried. "Why don't you just say you changed your mind?"

"I can't," she replied. "They asked other people already!"

I sighed. Emily was cute and overly nice, so I was still convinced she could find a date.

"Why don't you ask a junior?" I offered.

"I guess I could, but I want to go with someone I like," she said.

"Harrison, could you go into the kitchen for a sec?" I asked him.

"Sure," he said and walked off, likely relieved to remove himself from such girly talk, and probably hungry as always.

I motioned to Emily to sit down.

"Who?" I asked.

"What?" she returned.

"Who, do you like?" I clarified.

"It doesn't matter," she said. "He is going with someone else, and he never asked me to start with."

I decided not to push it, because it sort of sounded like a lost cause.

"And you don't like any of the juniors?" I asked.

"Not really, no," she said and I sighed again.

"Well, you could just show up and dance with a bunch of different guys," I suggested in an attempt to cheer her up.

"Taylor, thanks for the lessons and everything, but I think I am going to go home now," Emily said. She got up from the couch, grabbed her purse and disappeared down the stairs. I felt like I should have gone after her, but I decided against it. It was her life, not mine, and if she didn't want to go to prom, I wasn't going to force her.

I went to retrieve Harrison from the kitchen.

"Well, that went well," I said sarcastically.

"At least she stepped on your toes and not mine," he said with a mouth full of food.

I punched him playfully in the arm.

KD Lee Writes

Chapter 17 - Prom

I brushed my hair out for the fifth time, since I put on the prom dress. It was a perfect fit. After Emily decided not to go to the prom, I had gone shopping with Kate and Jasmine. I had mistakably brought up Emily in one of our discussions, and they had shot me a nasty look like I had just told them that I liked to eat raw sea slugs at the beach or something equally as gross.

I quickly changed the subject, before they could go off on a rant about her. I still didn't get why they hated her so much; it made no sense. Plus, last year they weren't really the jealous types like Taffeta was. I thought about asking them why they disliked Emily so much, but that would only set them off. I changed my thoughts around to think about prom.

My first Prom—a once-or-twice in a lifetime opportunity! I was only getting to go as a junior since Harrison was a senior.

Harrison was picking me up ten minutes before prom started. The ride to the school was a lot quicker when the transportation wasn't a bus. He wasn't picking me up in a limo, though, either—he was picking me up in his car.

One: We didn't have the money for a limo.

Two: Even if we did have the money, I wouldn't want to waste it on something as stupid as a limo. Although, I would admit that I would like to ride in one at some point.

Three: Like I mentioned before, the drive was only ten minutes long, so it wasn't worth all the trouble anyway.

Harrison opened the passenger door for me, when we got there, and I got out of the car. There were balloons and a red carpet leading up to the door of the gym.

Harrison and I held hands and walked up to the gym. The gym was full of loud, blaring music from the band on the stage. The stage was decorated with streamers and balloons like the rest of the gym. The band that occupied it was singing an upbeat song, and already quite a few couples were going crazy on the dance floor.

"Do you want a drink?" Harrison asked, motioning to the table full of snacks and punch.

"Not really, let's dance," I said, pulling him onto the dance floor as the band switched to another song. It was a really old one, but it was still fun—it was called "Let's Twist Like We Did Last Summer."

A girl bumped into me, and I turned around. It was Jasmine, and she was dancing with Chad.

"Sorry, oh, hey, Taylor!" she said. "You look great!"

"You too!" I replied. Jasmine's dress was a dazzling blue.

I would have considered buying the dress myself, if it didn't show so much cleavage. She looked better in it than I would have anyway. The blue went so well with her hair and skin tone.

I went back to dancing with Harrison. Besides seeing him dance while we were trying and failing at teaching Emily how to dance, I'd never seen him dance before. Most guys were awkward on the dance floor, but Harrison almost looked like he had taken lessons. I couldn't imagine him doing that though.

"Have you taken dance lessons?" I asked.

He chuckled, quietly.

"No, not exactly, my parents love to dance and they taught me how when I was a kid," he said. That explains a lot.

I had heard that lots of people were going to a party at Asher's after prom. I decided to ask Harrison about it.

"Are you planning on going to the party after?" I asked Harrison. I hoped he'd rather go out to eat or something. As it turned out, that was exactly what he had in mind, thanks to his never ending appetite.

"I was thinking I could take you to Miller's Ale House," he said. "Do you want to go?"

Miller's Ale House was a chain restaurant. The closest one was only a couple miles from the airport, which was fairly close to the high school.

Harrison loved their food. He normally ordered the meal of 35 shrimp and fries. I didn't know how he could eat so much. Personally, I would have puked. I usually got the fish tacos or a burger. They had the best fish tacos in Florida, in my opinion.

"Sure," I replied.

Then, I spotted Emily in the corner of room. She must have come stag! I couldn't believe she actually came!

"Harrison, look!" I said. "Emily came," he turned around and followed my gaze before his eyes could find her.

"I'm glad she could make it," he said.

"Let's go talk to her," I grabbed his hand, and we weaved through the crowd of people.

Emily really did look stunning. Her red hair sat pinned up on the back of her head, just above her long neck. A few loose strands of hair hung out of the bun on either side of her face. The silver dress she wore sparkled in the lighting.

"Emily!" I said, pulling her into a hug.

I was glad to see that she had decided on flat shoes instead of high heels. Emily plus high heels would equal disaster (or sore feet, and not just her feet would be sore).

"You should have told me you were coming!" I scolded. "I didn't even know you got a dress."

"It was kind of a snap decision, and the dress is left over from homecoming," she said.

"Who did your hair?" I asked.

"I did," she said, touching the bun self-consciously.

"It looks awesome!" I complimented her. "We are going out to eat at Miller's Ale House after. Do you want to come or are you going to the party?"

"If you guys don't mind…" she trailed off, and her eyes flicked towards Harrison.

"Of course not!" he said. "So you're in?"

"Sure," she said. We agreed to leave in another half-hour.

Harrison and I danced for a little longer, before Kate showed up. She was arm and arm with Kevin, a football player. I wondered what happened to Alex; they used to date.

"Hey, Taylor!" She greeted.

Kevin merely nodded at us.

"Hi Kate," I said.

"So, you guys going to Asher's party, later?" she asked.

"I think we are planning on going to Miller's Ale House," I replied.

"You guys mind some company?" she asked.

I grimaced.

"I don't think that is such a great idea," I said.

Before I could explain or Kate could question me, Emily showed up.

"Ready to go?" she asked. She stopped talking when she noticed, Kate.

"Oh, I see," Kate said. "You invited *her.*"

Kate stormed off, leaving Emily and me staring at her, dumfounded. Kevin shrugged before following her.

"What was that about?" Emily asked. I just shook my head.

"Let's get going," I said.

***

The car ride to Miller's Ale House was pretty quiet. Emily seemed quieter than usual, and I hoped that what Kate had said hadn't gotten to her.

At the restaurant, Emily ordered the fish tacos just like me. She said she had never tried them. I could hardly believe her; it was one of their most popular menu items!

Even after we left the restaurant, and Emily went home, Harrison continued to act like a real gentleman. He kissed me goodnight, but didn't push for anything else. I waved goodbye as he pulled out of the driveway.

KD Lee Writes

Olympic Bound

Summer

KD Lee Writes

Olympic Bound

CHAPTER 18 – LABYRINTH OF LIGHT

I packed two swimsuits, a swim cap, goggles, clothes, and a book into my suitcase. Mom had been rushing around all day getting everything ready and packing to fly out to Omaha, Nebraska for the Qualifications. It was summer now, so I didn't have to worry about missing class.

Harrison was flying out with us, too. Despite all of my support, I was extremely nervous. I had been swimming faster than the minimum qualifying times, so I hoped I would be able to keep that up at the Qualifications and make it to Trials. As I was packing, Mom hurried into my bedroom, frantic.

"Have you seen my red scarf?" she asked.

I shook my head.

"Why would you need a scarf?" I asked. "It is in the seventies in Omaha right now!" It was like she thought anywhere outside of Florida was a frozen wasteland or something.

"Right," Mom said. "Well, I guess I'll just leave it here, then" she said, turning back to her room.

I zipped up my suitcase, rolled it to the corner, and put my purse on top of it.

We would leave bright and early tomorrow morning before the sun even had time to wake up. From the airport in Omaha, we would take a rental car to the hotel where we would be staying. The day after our arrival was the start of Qualifications. After I swam those races, we would return home.

Initially, Harrison's parents were going to drive us to the airport, but my Aunt Libby offered to drive us at the last minute. Mom took her up on the offer, since she had just gotten back into the country from volunteering abroad and hadn't been able to visit with her. We rarely ever got to see her because she was always so busy traveling to other countries to help people in need.

For example, there was a tsunami in Japan, and she was one of the first volunteers to go over there. She also helped feed starving people in Africa. Another time, she went to India. I can't remember why she went there, though.

Olympic Bound

I was very excited about Qualifications, but another thing I couldn't wait for was getting to fly on a plane. It would be my first plane ride.

I didn't think I would be nervous; it was way more likely that one would die in a car crash than in a plane crash. It would be so thrilling to see the ground from so high up in the sky.

My phone rang, and I looked down at the caller ID. It was Harrison. I hit the ACCEPT button and put the phone to my ear.

"Hey, Harrison!" I greeted. "Are you all packed?"

"Yep, are you nervous?" he asked.

"About the flight or Qualifications?" I replied.

"Both," he said.

"I am nervous about Qualifications, but not the flight," I answered.

"So the reason I called is I wanted to ask how the car arrangement was going to work," he said. "Is Libby picking you guys up and then me? Or am I driving to your place, and will Libby pick us all up from there? Or how are we doing this?"

I told him that Libby would pick Mom and me up. Then the three of us would pick him up at his house. He thanked me before hanging up.

***

The next day, Harrison and all of us climbed quickly into Libby's car. Her alarm hadn't gone off at the right time and we were twenty minutes late. Great! Just great! I couldn't miss my flight!

She ran a few lights on the way, and I crossed my fingers that there weren't any cops. It turned out that there weren't any police around that early in the morning.

Libby parked in front of the airport, and we lugged our suitcases out of the trunk.

"Come on. Let's go! Thank you, Libby!" Mom exclaimed, racing up to the airport's sliding, glass doors.

I wheeled my suitcase behind me as we rushed inside. It had a squeaky wheel, and it whined in protest, as I rushed it to the check-in terminal. Mom had packed way too many things for our short trip, two suitcases and a purse for three days in Omaha? All she forgot was the kitchen sink (just kidding). Mom threw one of her bags on the scale.

The lady standing behind the counter shook her head. "Ma'am, this bag is five-pounds overweight," she said.

Mom cursed, under her breath, and she pulled it back off to take something out of it. She took out some clothes and put the suitcase back on the scale.

"Now it is three-pounds overweight," the lady recited.

Mom balled her hands into fists and pulled the suitcase, roughly, back onto the floor, throwing the clothes back in and putting it back on the scale.

"How much will it cost to take it as is?" Mom asked.

"Seventy-five dollars, extra," the counter attendant replied, bluntly.

"Seventy-five!" Mom gasped, before pulling the suitcase off (again!) and dragging out a few books. She put it back on the scale. FINALLY, it was down to the right weight.

"What will I do with these books?" she asked.

"There is a trash can right over there," the lady replied, while pointing across the way.

Mom took a deep breath to keep her cool and not jump across the scale to strangle the lady right then and there.

"Mom, we have to go," I reminded her.

"Fine," she said, through clenched teeth. We checked the other bag as well.

"Since you are so late in getting here, we can't guarantee that your bags will get to the airport in Omaha when you do," the attendant informed us.

"JUST . . . get them there," Mom said, balling her fists again and struggling to keep her cool.

I stared at the vein bulging in her neck. We got our boarding passes, and Mom dramatically dropped the books into the trash can.

I grabbed her hand and dragged her behind me, trying to rush her. Didn't she realize that we were running out of time?

After getting through security, we got to the door just as they were about to close it. I stuck my hand in the door.

"I . . . Need . . . To . . . Get . . . On. . . That . . . Flight!" I said, stressing each word, emphatically.

"Let me see your boarding passes," he said. We showed them to him, and he waved us through. Phew! That was a close call. Too close!

We rushed down the hallway, and I stumbled onto the plane, almost running into a pretty flight attendant.

"Watch your step," she warned me.

A little late for that wasn't it?

We put our luggage overhead and sat down in our seats. Mom got the window, I got the middle, and Harrison got the aisle. I stuck my head in front of Mom's and peered out the window.

Olympic Bound

We weren't moving yet, but I tried to imagine what it would look like when we finally got in the air. Breathtaking, I hoped. Or maybe not. Maybe the scenery would be a disappointment. I doubted it though. It would probably be everything I hoped for.

Harrison grabbed my hand and held it in his lap. I squeezed it back.

"Are you afraid of flying?" I asked.

He shook his head.

"No," he said. "I have been on a plane a few times before, and like you said, people are more likely to die in a car crash than a plane crash."

"Well, I'm excited," I said. "What does the view look like from the air?"

"Like a bunch of tiny lights and terrain," he replied.

The plane pulled away from the terminal, and we turned around and started slowly down the taxiway. Then, turning a second time, we lined up on the runway. After a brief pause, the plane started to quickly pick up speed. I squeezed Harrison's hand tighter.

"You sure you're alright?" he asked.

"Positive," I replied. The front wheels came up off the tarmac, and before I knew it, so did the back wheels.

Suddenly, we were in the air. I stared past Mom out the window again.

"Your hair is in my face," she said, crossly.

I pulled my hair over one shoulder, but I didn't move. My eyes stayed glued to the view outside the window.

The ground started to shrink below us. Yes, there were lights, but I could see houses and cars stretching out below us. The world shrank some more as we ascended higher and higher into the air.

The world looked beautiful from this view, but it also looked sad. I was sure most people wouldn't view it like that, but I could imagine what the world must have looked like from this point of view hundreds of years ago, before there were cars, high-rises, pollution, and more artificial lighting than you could imagine.

CHAPTER 19 - ANTICIPATION

One of the flight attendants took our drink orders. I ordered a Coke and Harrison ordered Sprite. Mom went with a Bud Light, even after I scolded her. What was she thinking? She was a recovering alcoholic. Or somewhat recovering, anyway.

"Mom!" I admonished.

"Just one," she said and nodded to the flight attendant to let her know she was still getting the beer.

I shook my head furiously.

Mom changed the subject like she usually did.

"Anyway, aren't you excited?" she asked. "Olympic Trials here we come!"

Again I had to correct her.

"Mom, this is the Qualifications for the Trials," I reminded her.

"But I thought you did Qualifications at home in that swim meet," she said.

"No. That was to get into Qualifications," I replied.

How many times did I have to explain it to her?

"Trials are a lot bigger of a deal," I continued. "If I get first or second place in Trials, I will be going to the Olympics."

"Gosh, there are a lot of steps!" she exclaimed.

At least that statement was true; there were a lot of steps to get into the Olympics.

"Is there going to be a crowd?" she asked.

I shrugged.

"Just family and friends of the girls that are trying to qualify," I said.

I looked up Qualifications on YouTube and all the videos showed just a bunch of people sitting or standing around the pool. In the videos of Trials, there were way more people—a whole stadium of people that bought tickets to see the event, in fact.

The flight attendant made her way back down the aisle and handed us our drinks. I shook my head, disapprovingly, at the drink that sat on top of Mom's tray.

"Just one!" she barked again.

I hoped so. I couldn't have her drunk during Qualifications.

"It is a celebratory drink," she explained. "I am so proud of you! You know that right?"

I nodded. Mom didn't say that very often, so I was a little taken aback.

I leaned into Harrison and rested my head on his shoulder. I didn't normally sleep well when I traveled, but, before I knew it, I was fast asleep.

***

I woke up as one of the flight attendants took our empty cups and dumped them in a trash bag. I tried to fall back to sleep, but it was nearly impossible. We had been at cruising altitude for a while and were surrounded by clouds, so I couldn't enjoy the view.

Instead, I pulled out my phone and flipped through a series of encouraging texts from classmates.

Haylee: U rock girl! ☺

Ava: Have fun in Omaha Ne! You will do great!

Sunny: you are the best swimmer on our team! you'll get in, don't worry.

Emily: call me when you get in, i want to hear all about it! I would wish u good luck but you don't need it! ☺

Jasmine: Good Luck!!!

Kate: U will do gr8!

I looked over at Mom and discovered that she was sleeping with her head resting on the window. Harrison was awake still, so I talked with him.

"Do you think I will get in?" I asked.

"Of course!" he replied, immediately. "You have been swimming faster than the minimum qualifying time every practice for the past month. Don't let it get in your head that you might not maintain that time. You will."

I was already nervous, though, but I didn't say anything to Harrison about that. What if something happened and I didn't even make it to Trials? That would be an immense disappointment. Don't even get me started on Trials. That wasn't going to be a piece of cake, if I even made it that far. Those thoughts tired me out, so I leaned back into Harrison and fell asleep once again.

***

Olympic Bound

There was a one-hour time difference in Omaha, so even though it was 9:00 A.M. in Florida, it was 8:00 A.M. when we landed in Omaha.

All of us grabbed what luggage we hadn't checked and headed down to get the two bags we had checked from baggage claim. After walking to the bottom of the escalator, we waited for our bags at the luggage carrousel.

A green bag came out first and began to circle on the conveyor belt. Not ours. Then a black one and a purple one came down the conveyor belt. Again, not ours. After twenty bags had come out, none of which were ours, we began to worry.

The desk agent at the Florida airport had said that she might not be able to get our bags to Nebraska with us. After we waited for about fifteen more minutes, during which time every bag was taken off the carrousel, Mom stormed up to the desk.

"Where are my bags?" she asked, furiously.

"Please calm down, Ma'am. What is your name?" The attendant asked.

"Emma Reeve," she huffed.

He typed something into his computer, as Mom handed him the slips of paper we had gotten with our tickets to claim any baggage that didn't make it to Nebraska.

"It looks like your bags are in Fort Myers, Florida," he said.

"Why aren't they here?!" She asked, angrily.

"It looks like we weren't able to get them on the flight in time for departure," he explained.

"Why couldn't you make time?!" she asked.

The guy heaved a sigh. "Ma'am, I am sorry that your bags didn't get here when you hoped they would, but it isn't really my fault," he said. "They will be here on the next flight, and we can have them delivered to your place. Is that ok?"

"Um, yes, only we are going to be staying at a hotel," she replied.

He typed something in his computer.

"What is the address?" he asked.

"I don't know, I will have to call," Mom said and pulled out her phone. She looked up the number online, called the hotel, and repeated the address and room number back to him.

"Ok, got it," he said. "Your bags will be delivered to you by tomorrow."

Mom clenched her fists again and nodded.

"Alright-y then, let's go," Mom said, forcing a smile.

Olympic Bound

I grabbed her hand and led her away, not bothering to point out if she had just brought a carry-on like Henry and I, none of this would have happened.

We went down to the bottom floor and rented a cheap car for the next three days. We got inside, and Mom turned on the air conditioning. It was 90 degrees outside.

The fan for the air conditioning didn't even turn on. Mom just shook her head as if to say: *'Of course it doesn't work!'* and buckled her seatbelt.

I took the passenger seat next to Mom and Harrison took the back seat. At least the car started. Next stop was our hotel room.

***

"We're here," Mom said, pointing out the obvious just like Mel used to do. Our hotel was small, but it looked like it would be clean and cozy. Harrison pulled my suitcase from the trunk, and I pulled the handle out, dragging it behind me.

The hotel was three floors high, so after picking up our keycard we took the elevator instead of the stairs. Man, the suitcases were so heavy!

We swiped the card and walked into the room. There were three twin beds arranged side-by-side. We saw a small refrigerator, a counter, a microwave, a dresser, a closet, and a bathroom filled with mini shampoos and hand soaps.

I thought about unpacking my clothes into the dresser, but then decided against it. That thing had probably never been washed (unless you count dusting).

"Well this is nice," Mom said.

"Tiny," I replied, not meaning to sound so ungrateful.

Mom couldn't afford anything better than this, and at least there weren't cockroaches crawling up out of the sink or bedbugs in the sheets. At least I hopped there wasn't-I hadn't actually checked, yet.

Just to make sure, I looked around in the bathroom and pulled the quilt back from one of the twin beds. They passed my little health inspection, thank goodness.

"Let's go eat somewhere," Harrison said. I looked at the clock on the nightstand.

"Harrison it is 9:05 A.M.," I told him. What do you want? Breakfast?"

"I'm guessing Nebraska has a Denny's," Harrison said.

"I'm guessing this hotel serves breakfast, too," Mom said. "Let's see."

Olympic Bound

Sure enough, the hotel served breakfast, but it was your typical soggy waffle, stale cereal, and dry muffin hotel continental-style breakfast.

Even still, Harrison ate like he would never see food again. I kind of did too for that matter; we hadn't had enough time to eat breakfast at home before we left for the airport.

After breakfast, we made sure we knew where the Qualifications were being held, so we could go straight there tomorrow. The GPS on my phone would take us right to the natatorium complex.

Tomorrow I would get to find out if I was going to Trials right in that very building!

KD Lee Writes

Olympic Bound

CHAPTER 20 - QUALIFICATIONS

Mom's bags still hadn't arrived the next morning, and it was almost time to take off for Qualifications. "Let's just go," Mom eventually moaned.

I squealed excitedly. I had my swimsuit under my clothes and my cap and goggles in hand.

We got in the car and made our way to the building. It was only seven minutes from our hotel. I sat in the back with Harrison.

"What if we came all this way for nothing?" I asked. "I mean, we paid for the flights, and Mom, you had to take off work. What if this was all just a big waste of time?"

"You will make it!" Harrison said. "Don't worry about it! You've got this."

I nodded my head, trying to convince myself he was right.

"Yeah, you're right," I said.

"Of course I am," he said, before leaning in and kissing me.

When we pulled away, I caught Mom's eye in the rearview mirror.

Awkward…

***

I had to wait in what was called the "ready room" while girls competed before me.

All of the girls around me were either on the phone, listening to music, stretching, taking deep breaths to calm themselves, or some other activity trying to remain composed. One girl in the corner was even crying. Maybe she was overwhelmed by nerves? She blew her nose constantly on soft tissues.

Another one of the girls was sitting next to her trying to comfort her, but was doing a poor job of it. Every time she said something, the crying girl sobbed even harder.

I decided to do a few stretches myself—ones that Coach Hamton had given me, just so I could loosen up. As I stretched, the crying girl continued carrying on. The girl who was once trying to comfort the crying girl moved away, so I stopped stretching and crept over to her.

"Is she ok?" I asked.

"Not really," the girl said. "Her dad is really hard on her. She has been training her whole life. If she doesn't make it past Qualifications, her dad will freak! She is so terrified she won't make it through. If I make it through and she doesn't, her dad will give her an especially hard time, since she and I are training partners. I don't know why she is so worried. She is a great swimmer! Anyway, I'm Ava and her name is Penny. What is your name?"

"I'm Taylor," I answered. I didn't want talk anymore, so I quickly said my goodbyes and wished the girl luck.

I resumed stretching. Penny blew her nose for the twentieth time and stuck in her earbuds. I wished Harrison was here, but he had gone with Mom to watch the girls who were competing before me.

I reached down to touch my toes, and then I did a few shoulder rolls, first to the front and then to the back.

One girl in the corner was doing a handstand and leaning upside down against the wall. Weird. She had her shirt tucked in, too.

"What are you doing?" someone asked her.

I looked around the "ready room" to the girl doing the handstand. She looked to be the youngest one there. She looked like she was maybe thirteen. She was tall, but her young face gave away her age.

"I am getting more blood into my head," the girl answered, simply.

The girl who had asked the question just shrugged and sat down, watching each girl, intently. First, she watched Penny, then another girl who was doing jumping jacks, and then another girl who was listening to music.

She looked bored sitting there with nothing do, just waiting to swim. She didn't look nervous at all. She started drumming on her knees until finally her eyes fell on me.

"Hi," she said.

"Hello," I replied, coolly.

"Are you nervous?" she asked.

"A little," I replied.

"Not me," she said, even though I hadn't asked her a question. "I am making it to Trials no matter what."

"How do you know that?" I questioned.

"A fortune teller told me," she replied.

Olympic Bound

Well, at least she was confident. That was good, I guessed.

"How old are you?" I asked her.

I was surprised by what she said next.

"Twelve," she replied.

Wow! That was really young to be trying to get into the Olympics! But there was no age limit in Olympic swimming, unlike in gymnastics.

"Wow, well, good luck!" I told her.

"You too," she said, breaking into a big smile.

I looked at the clock. It was almost time for me to compete.

***

I dove into the water, barely making a splash as I broke through the surface. I jetted like a torpedo before breaking into a freestyle stroke. This was my first event: the 50-meter freestyle.

I kicked my legs as fast as I could and propelled myself forward with my arms. I did not know how I was doing on time, or how I was doing compared to the rest of the girls, but I hoped it was good enough to qualify.

I wanted this so bad. Not just for me, not just for the memory of my Dad—who wanted this for me more than anyone—but for Mel, whose death prompted Mom to let me swim again.

I reached the other end of the pool and looked up at the time. I had made it! Even though I had come in second place, I qualified to go to the Olympic Trials for the 50-meter freestyle! I looked to see who had beaten me. It was Penny, the girl who had been in the "ready room" crying. She was pumping her fists in the air.

I decided to mimic Penny by throwing my fists into the air, before pulling myself out of the pool and joining Harrison and Mom in the stands.

"You did it!" Mom cried, kissing me on the cheek.

Harrison joined me in a high-five.

"Good job, Taylor!" he cried.

"Don't forget," I said, "I still have the 100 freestyle, the 50 breaststroke, the 100 breaststroke, and the 200 and 400 medley,"

"You got them in the bag," Harrison insisted.

"I hope so," I replied.

Mom wrapped me in a towel and I watched the next few competitions until it was time for me to do the 100-meter freestyle.

I stood on the starting block and crouched down. Time slowed down. I needed to win. I thought over everything I needed to do. I couldn't dive into the water too soon, since the block could detect a false start. I started with my back leg at a 90-degree angle to optimize the power of my launch.

For this race, I had two laps to complete, so I had to make sure I got my turn just right. I wasn't too worried about that part, though. I had mastered that. What I needed to worry about was speed.

I thought about how I needed to maximize my acceleration off the starting block. I grabbed the front of the starting block, so I could push with my hands as well as my feet. I thought about how I needed to pull up on the block to increase the frictional force on my feet so my legs could help propel me.

As soon as I heard the sound of the starting gun, I pushed off and broke into freestyle stroke, cupping my hands for maximum speed. Before long, I reached the other side and did a flip-turn, kicking off the cement wall with as much force as I could muster.

I kept my hands out in front of me, shooting through the water, until I reached the surface again. I spun my arms around like a windmill and turned my head to the right side every second stroke to breathe.

Before I knew it, I was at the wall again. I came in first place this time! First place!

Many people I didn't know congratulated me for getting first, including Mom and Harrison. Afterward, I had to wait a long time before the 100-meter breaststroke. There wasn't a 50-meter breaststroke race.

When the breaststroke series of races were up, I was placed in the second group of competitors. I watched the girls compete before me. Ava was in the first group, and I watched her flawless technique. She was a lot better with the breaststroke than the other ones.

Before I knew it, I was back on the starting block in the ready position. My heart raced, and I clenched and unclenched my fists to get rid of some of the anxiety.

Breaststroke was not my strong stroke, and I knew it, but I still wanted to qualify. I dove into the water and swam like a frog down to the end of the pool and back.

Amazingly, I finished in fourth place! Fourth! I took a deep breath and shook off my anxiety.

Harrison gave me a thumbs' up from the stands. I returned the gesture, before pulling myself out of the water. I still had to swim three more races.

Lucy wasn't competing in the 100-meter breaststroke, but Penny was. She had competed in all of them so far, all of them! I questioned Ava to see how many more Penny would be doing.

"Her dad is making her do all of them," Ava replied.

Olympic Bound

I shook my head with disbelief. She would be too tired to qualify in the last ones, wouldn't she? I couldn't help but feel sympathy for her; her dad must have been really hardcore!

As it turned out, Penny didn't meet the Qualifications time for breaststroke. I watched her pull herself out of the water, sadly, with her head down.

Poor Penny! I really felt bad for her. She made her way slowly to the stands on the opposite side of the pool where Harrison, Mom, and I were sitting.

Her dad began yelling at her right off, careful not to raise his voice too loud to draw attention to himself. He wasn't doing a great job of it, though. People turned in their seats to watch the fallout. I tried to read Penny's lips.

"Daddy . . . I didn't—" stammered Penny, before her father cut her off. He had his back to me, so I couldn't hear what he was saying. But it must not have been good, because tears spring up to Penny's eyes.

Her dad clenched his fists, but didn't use them. Instead he sat down, angrily, and put his hands up in a shushing gesture when Penny tried to say something.

She wiped her eyes and turned her head to the swimming pool. I looked away and got ready to swim again. My group was up next.

For this race, I had four laps to complete. I was good at swimming for long stretches. I ended up getting sixth place after all of the groups swam.

In the water, I tried to think of nothing but my strokes. Visions of Penny and her dad flash in my mind, though. I tried to push them away, but I kept seeing her sad face. Was she physically abused, too? I mean, not just emotionally?

After my first lap, I succeeded in pushing those thoughts away and focused on only swimming and keeping in tune with the water around me. It killed me not to know if I was doing well. I was not quite sure how many girls were ahead of me.

I finished my second lap and spun around to complete my third. *Almost there!* I thought as I approached the pool wall. I swiveled around for my last lap.

I didn't even feel winded as I finished the race. I was in third place this time. I pumped my fists in the air and joined Harrison and Mom in the stands again.

Just then, I realized what all this meant. I was going to the Olympic Trials! I had a fighting chance to make it to the Olympics! If only I could work between now and the Trials to make sure to get first or second place in every competition. . . .

I felt like I was practically glowing. I looked at Lucy, who radiated the same happiness I did. She was making it to

Olympic Bound

Trials as well, and so were Ava, Penny, Joy, and several others. I would have to beat all of them or all but one at least.

KD Lee Writes

Olympic Bound

CHAPTER 21 — GOOD LUCK

"You're going to Trials, do you realize that?!" Harrison howled joyfully, hugging me tightly.

"I know, I know!" I shouted back, even though we were sitting right next to each other.

"Whoop-whoop-hooray for Taylor!" Mom bellowed.

Lucy (who qualified for 50-meter freestyle, 100-meter freestyle, and 200-meter medley) made her way over to me.

"You were amazing!" she expressed, a little dreamily.

I got third on 50-meter freestyle (at first I had second place, but not after everyone competed), first on the 100-meter freestyle, sixth on the 100-meter breaststroke, fifth on the 200-meter breaststroke, eighth on the 200-meter medley and seventh on the 400-meter medley.

"What do you mean?" I asked. "You're twelve and you're going to Trials! The USA *Olympic* Swimming Trials!" I reminded her.

"Yeah, but I only just qualified for three of them," she cried. "You qualified for six! One of them you came in first!"

"Thanks! Anyway, high-five! Good job, Lucy," I said to her, giving her a hard high-five.

"See you at Trials!" she shouted.

"See you at Trials!" I yelled back. She was a sweet girl.

Her family looked very supportive as well. She had her brother, mom, dad, and grandma with her. I saw where she got her height from, too. Each one of them was tall. Even her grandma looked like she was six feet tall! Oh, and the dad—he was a giant at almost seven feet tall! Ava's mom was crying tears of joy and hugging her fiercely.

Just then, Mom pulls me into a hug. "I am so proud of you," she exclaimed, and she started to cry, too.

I wondered if she was thinking about Dad. She answered my suspicion in the next heartbeat.

"Your father would be so proud of you," she assured me.

Olympic Bound

Finally, Harrison joined the group and hugged me. Then we just stood there wiping joyful tears from our eyes.

"Who's hungry?" Harrison asked.

Mom and I laughed. On our way to the car, Lucy chased us down.

"Taylor!" she shouted. I swiveled around to look at her.

"I have something for you!" she said, opening a fist to reveal a shiny brownish stone. She dropped it into my hand.

"It will give you good luck," she said. I closed my fist around the gem.

"Thanks, Lucy," I replied.

"Just keep it with you wherever you go," she suggested, before running back to join her parents.

It was obvious she was into all that voodoo stuff. The fortune teller, the lucky stones—it was all part of what she believed in. I stuck the stone in my pocket and grabbed Harrison's hand and continued walking to the car.

I looked up good restaurants in the area. Siri took a while to figure out I was not in Florida anymore, but finally, she came up with a list of four-and-a-half-to-five-star restaurants. I picked one called Stan's

Steakhouse, and Siri pulled up a map showing directions for how to get to the restaurant.

***

The food was delicious; the mashed potatoes with gravy were the best mashed potato dish that I had ever had. It was a great way to end the day!

After eating, we headed back to the hotel. We arrived just as the airport porter was knocking on the door with Mom's suitcases. What good timing.

"Oh, are you Mrs. Reeve?" he asked. She nodded.

"Sorry for the mix up at the airport," he continued. "Here are your bags."

Mom took them and the airport porter bounded down the stairs. He didn't even ask for proof that Mom was Emma Reeve! Why had he just handed over the luggage so fast without some identification? What if she wasn't who she said she was? I stopped worrying and followed Harrison and Mom into the hotel room. The important thing was that Mom got her bags back.

***

In the morning, we drove to the airport and dropped off our car before getting into the security-check line.

After taking off our shoes and placing them on the conveyor belt in little gray tubs, we walked one by one through the metal detector. Mom and I got through fine, but when Harrison went through, the detector beeped. He was asked to stop.

"Oh! My belt! Wait a sec," Harrison said and slipped off his belt. He put it in a conveyor belt tub, before walking back through the detector again.

"Ok, you're alright," the TSA agent said, waving him on.

We grabbed our things and continued on to the flight. We had come extra early this time to make sure we avoided an incident like last time. That may have been a mistake, though, because now we had to sit in the airport for an hour and a half with nothing to do.

Just as I was thinking that, I looked up at the screens displaying departure times only to see that the flight traveling to Fort Myers, Florida had been delayed. Now it was rescheduled to leave at 2:15 P.M. —two-and-a-half-hours later than expected! Great, scratch my last comment. Now we have to sit around for four hours!

"I guess we could go to Subway," Mom offered. I shrugged.

"I think I'll get a coffee," I said, as I stood up. "You guys want anything?"

Harrison stood up, too.

"I'll go with you," he said.

"Could you get me a Carmel Frappuccino?" Mom asked.

I nodded, before walking off, hand in hand with Harrison.

Once we were out of view of Mom, Harrison pulled me into him and French kissed me right there in the middle of the airport! But I didn't feel those butterflies that I usually did. Normally, I never wanted such a moment to end. But now I was waiting for him to just finish up already.

Did that mean we were growing apart? It seemed like we had been getting farther and farther from each other since summer began. Or maybe it was just me who was feeling removed from him.

Harrison must have been able to tell that something was wrong, because he pulled away.

"What?" he asked.

I really didn't know what. But it seemed as though I had been lying to myself and Harrison for some time. Mostly because Harrison had never done anything wrong. He had been nothing but supportive. The problem was me, and I didn't even know why.

"I'm just thirsty," I said, dismissively. "Let's grab those coffees."

We reached the Starbucks, and Harrison insisted on paying for both Mom's and my Frappuccino, as well has his Cappuccino and a cookie. I sipped my coffee, and we walked back to Mom.

"Four hours," Mom mumbled, more to herself than us, while shaking her head. "I guess it makes up for us not having to wait at all for the flight getting here." Mom shrugged.

"I guess," I agreed, plopping down next to her and handing her coffee to her.

***

The flight back home seemed shorter than the flight to Nebraska, but that might just be in my head. Now it would be back to training. Lots of training! Based on the times I swam at the Qualifications, I would have only made it to the Olympics in two events. I have to do better than that.

Emily had agreed to train with me every day. She was a great swimmer. Not Olympic material necessarily, but good, nonetheless.

"I can't believe you are going to the Olympics!" Emily cried, excitedly, when I saw her after we got back from Nebraska.

"I hope so, but I don't know yet," I replied, reminding her I was not going just yet.

"You are, I can feel it, and I can tell by watching you swim," she replied.

Olympic Bound

Senior

Year

KD Lee Writes

Chapter 22 – Bad Luck

"It really hurts," I whimpered through tears.

"I think we should go to the emergency room," Mom judged, picking up my hand to examine it.

I winced in pain.

"I think your wrist is broken," Mom said.

I guess I should probably fill you in on what just happened. I broke my wrist doing a handstand. Yeah, a handstand! How does that even happen? I will tell you how.

There was an exercising unit at the park that I had been going to for cross training. It had pull up bars, balance beams, and other equipment as well as two upside-down U's in the ground to stretch your calves.

If I had been smart, I would have stretched my calves on it. Instead I grabbed onto the two U's and did a handstand on them.

But . . . my right hand slipped and landed on the cement underneath, which caused me to lose my balance. I fell backwards and snapped my wrist in the U about the same time my back hit the concrete.

After which, my wrist felt like it was on fire and my back felt like it is made of one big bruise. To top it all off, we had to walk a mile to get back to the car. One good smidgen of luck was that mom had decided to join me that day.

Mom helped me to my feet and I limped along beside her in our quest to the car. I extended my fingers and stopped straight away. I was almost positive it was broken.

What about swimming!? How could I swim with a broken wrist?! How could I practice for Trials!? Trials were only three months and twenty days away! It had been over half a year since qualifiers, and I had been training hard for hours every day.

"How is your back?" Mom asked.

It felt so bad. How long would a wrist take to heal anyway? A long time I thought—at least a month . . . maybe longer.

Olympic Bound

My old, friend Tami broke her wrist falling off the monkey bars, and I think that was about how long she had to have a cast. I remembered it so well because she couldn't swim with me for so long. She wasn't allowed to get her cast wet. Sure you can wrap your hand in plastic wrap for showers. But the doctors don't let you get into the pool. I gulped—*no swimming practice? What was I going to do about Trials?! My wrist can't be broken!*

It isn't broken. It isn't broken. It isn't broken, I chanted in my head as though just thinking it would make it come true. I seriously had the worst luck of anyone on the planet!

Maybe I should start keeping the brown stone that Lucy had given to me with me at all times! At that point, I would do anything to stop this string of bad luck!

Nothing ever turned out, except making it to Trials and hopefully to the Olympics. But that might be impossible now with a broken wrist.

I was right handed! How would I do a lot of things with only one left hand for a month? Seriously!

We made it to the car and Mom rushed me to the emergency room. After signing in and going through all the insurance stuff, a nurse grabbed me an icepack to hold on my wrist while we waited to be seen by a doctor.

I blinked back tears that still threatened to creep to the surface. I hadn't cried since Mel died, and before that I hadn't cried since my dad had died.

I didn't cry if I could help it. This felt like nothing compared to the pain I felt when Dad and Mel died. Yet, I had to take in the fact that it might have ruined my chances to go to the Olympics.

I definitely would have given up the chance to go to the Olympics, if I could get Mel or Dad back. I would give up a lot to get them back. But since I couldn't, I wanted to win the Olympics for them.

We sat in the waiting room for a long time. *So much for being speedy in the E.R.!* We remained there for nearly an hour before someone called my name.

"Taylor?" The lady summoned.

"Right here," I responded and followed her into a patient room.

"Hello, my name is Kelly," she said, shutting the door behind us.

"So tell me, what happened to your wrist?" Kelly asked.

"I . . . broke my wrist, or I think I broke it while doing a handstand," I told her.

"A handstand? How did that happen?" she asked.

I explained the whole scenario to Kelly, while she nodded and listened patiently.

"Well, I have never heard of anyone breaking a wrist doing a handstand, but there is a first for everything," she said. "Let's take an X-ray to make sure."

It didn't take long to find out that my wrist was truly broken, and for Kelly to wrap it in a cast.

"Excuse me, Kelly, but my daughter is competing in the USA Swimming Olympic Trials soon," Mom said. 'Will her wrist be healed by then?"

"I should be able to take this cast off in about two weeks, but it will have to have a brace for an additional four to six weeks," Kelly replied.

"What about swimming practice?" I asked. "Can I get my cast wet?"

"No, I am afraid you won't be able to swim while your wrist is broken," Kelly replied, solemnly.

"You can still take showers though," she said. Kelly then explained how to cover the cast with a plastic bag and seal the opening with a rubber band. But all I could focus on was the fact that I wouldn't be able to swim. I really wouldn't get to practice!

KD Lee Writes

Chapter 23 – New Distractions

"Your wrist is really broken?" Emily asked from the other end of the line.

"Yep," I replied.

"So, no swim practice?!" Emily practically screamed into the phone.

I had already told her that, but I thought she was just now grasping the idea.

"Nope, no swim practice," I confirmed. "But I will still be going to the gym every day to stay strong."

"How are you going to work out with a cast on?" she questioned.

"My mom has a friend who is a personal trainer," I said. "She said she would help me."

Even calling people felt different now because I had to hold the phone with my left hand. A lot of things were different, actually. Writing was practically a waste of time. Writing with my left hand made my words look like scribbles drawn by a two-year-old. But my wrist was too sore to write with my right hand, yet. You could make out what I was writing, but only barely. In a couple days, my wrist should be healed enough to write with my right hand again without wincing in pain.

I wished I was ambidextrous. That would have made this so much easier. Mom was working today, so I had literally nothing to do. I thought about calling Harrison, but I decided to go to the Lee County Library instead and pick out a few good books. I needed the distraction, and I loved reading.

I hadn't read much, since the flight back from Nebraska. It seemed like ages since I had qualified at Trials, but it really wasn't that long ago.

At least I could still drive with my cast. It might not be as safe, since I was practically driving one handed, and I had to shift gears with my left hand now, but I could drive just the same as before.

The library wasn't too far, but it wasn't close by any means. It was a twenty-minute drive each way, which summed up to forty minutes of driving time.

I made sure to pay extra attention when I drove, especially near the light where that semi-truck driver had run through it. This time, however, there were only a few semis, and the drivers were following the law. This was where I had lost Mel. This was where it had all happened. I managed to push the thought away and continued to the library.

As soon as I walked into the library, I calmed and wondered why I didn't come here more often. I loved the library. Each book had a new adventure to uncover or something new to learn.

I always thought it was amazing how some authors had a way with words. How could they come up with such rich and original ideas all the time?

Of course, not all books were good. With some, I wondered how they even wound up on the shelves, because they were so awful. But obviously someone reads them, or else the library wouldn't carry them. If there was anything I hated worse than pre-calculus, it had to be reading an unappealing book.

I sighed, as I stroked the spines of a group of books five shelves from the floor.

"Big reader?" asked a boy I hadn't noticed who was standing there. He was peeking around the shelf at me.

"Not exactly," I replied.

The thing I liked most about the library wasn't getting to read the books, I checked out, when I got home. What I loved was going through the shelves and reading the backs of books that I picked out to see what mysteries I might uncover.

"But who can beat free books, right?" the mysterious boy asked.

Exactly. I started to reply, but he was gone, before I got the chance to speak.

I turned my attention back to the books. Once I had found a total of ten books that interested me, I stacked them under my chin and set them on the checkout counter, before digging into my purse to find my library card.

After every book was checked out, I headed for the sliding doors, but my books started to slip out of my grasp and were on the floor even before I had time to react.

I crouched to pick them up when a hand reached down to help. I looked up only to see that same boy again. I hadn't noticed much about his looks before, but this close, I noticed he had ocean-blue eyes and side-combed, brown hair.

"Thanks," I murmured, standing up and reaching for the five books of mine that he held in his hands.

"Want me to help you carry these to your car?" he asked, eyeing my cast.

Olympic Bound

"That's alright, I'm ok," I replied.

"Your wrist is broken, and you just dropped all the books you were holding," he pointed out, like I didn't already know that. But he did have a point.

"Ok, um, if you don't mind," I conceded.

I thought of mentioning that I had a boyfriend, so he wouldn't get the wrong idea, but it was extremely unlikely I would ever see him again, anyway, so I just followed him meekly to the car.

"I'm Tim," he said.

"Taylor," I replied.

"So how did you break your wrist?" he questioned.

"Doing a double flip off a three story building," I said.

He gave me a weird look.

"That sounded a lot cooler than how I actually broke it," I said. "I broke it doing a handstand."

"How did you do that?" he asked.

"Long story," I replied.

He shrugged, changing the subject for me.

"So what school do you go to?" he asked.

"After summer break, I'm going to Alma College," I responded.

"Ah, college girl, I have yet another year of high school before I go to college. Why Alma?" he queried.

"I love to swim, and they have a good swimming program," I answered.

I decided not to bring up the Trials because that story required a lot of talk, and we only had a short walk to my car.

"Interesting, are you any good?" he asked.

I shrugged, being modest at first, but I wanted to see his reaction, so I decided to tell him about Trials, after all.

"Well, I am going to the USA Swimming Olympic Trials in two months, so, yeah," I said.

His mouth formed a round O and his eyes got wide.

"You are in the Olympics?" he asked, eagerly.

"No, I am going to Trials to get into the Olympics," I explained, not getting into the long version of the story. "This is my car," I said, motioning to the black Chevy.

I unlocked my car, and Tim set my books on the passenger seat. I realized then that he didn't have any books himself.

"Bye, Taylor, good luck in the Trials!" he said and walked back towards the library.

It surprised me that he didn't ask for my phone number or anything, but I was relieved that I didn't have to make up an excuse to say no.

But that reminded me that I had to talk to Harrison. He was already going to college, and after the summer, I would be going to a different one. A long-distance relationship didn't seem appealing to me.

There just wasn't that magical spark between us anymore. At the same time, I felt terrible about it. He had just flown out to Nebraska with me. Could I really just end our relationship like that?

But then I remembered the lack of butterflies I had at the airport when he kissed me. It really wasn't fair to either of us, if I let this relationship drag out any further.

I had to end it now, before I changed my mind. Before I started up the car, I called Harrison.

"Hey, Taylor, what's up?" he said.

"Hi, Harrison, could I come over?" I asked. "I want to talk to you about something."

"I have to talk to you about something, too," he said grimly, so grimly that I wondered if something was seriously wrong.

"Err, ok, see you in an hour?" I asked.

"Ok, see you soon," he said.

I hung up and gripped onto the steering wheel with my left hand. What if his grandma had died or something like that? Could I really break up with him just after something horrible happened?

The anticipation was killing me, so I started up the car, left the library parking lot, and headed for Harrison's house.

I hit all the green lights, so I arrived earlier than I had expected. I braced myself and rehearsed the speech I was preparing to give him. But if the reason he wanted to talk to me was because something terrible had happened, I knew I wouldn't be able to go through with the break-up.

Harrison opened the door and I followed him inside. I decided I would let him start, so I would know whether it was a good time to dump him.

"You first," I instructed.

"Go ahead," he urged me.

"Could you go first?" I pleaded.

He took a deep breath.

Chapter 24 - Murderer

"You know I love you," he started.

I stared, astonished. He was breaking up with me? Really? That was the last thing I expected!

"You're breaking up with me?" I asked.

"It is the best thing for both of us," he said. "I will be going back to college soon and you will be going to Alma; I just think it would be best."

"I think you are completely right!" I said, a little too enthusiastically.

"Um, what?" he asked, confused.

"I was thinking the same thing," I explained. "That's what I wanted to talk to you about."

"Oh," he looked disappointed. "I am glad we feel the same." His words sounded forced.

"But could we still be friends?" I asked.

I didn't want to never, ever see him again. I loved him, but more as a close friend than as a boyfriend. We had been through so much together.

"Yeah, course," he said, sadly.

If he was the one who initiated the break-up, then why was he so sad? Did he want me to cry hysterically, insisting that we could make it work, and beg him to stay with me while I hyperventilated waiting for an answer?

We sat in silence for a while, neither of us making a move to say anything. After a few awkward minutes, I couldn't stand it anymore.

"I am glad we are still friends, Harrison," I said, standing up to hug him, before escaping out the front door.

He just sat there looking dumfounded and completely speechless.

A few salty tears clouded my vision, but I didn't cry. Like normal, I saved my tears for something much more worthy. I shouldn't be crying about breaking up with my boyfriend. I should only cry if he broke up with me.

But he did, I reminded myself. He broke up with me, so it was normal to cry, right? At that thought I let one single, lonely, tear travel down my cheek and around my chin.

It traveled down my neck. It tickled, so I wiped it away before it could inflict any more damage. But after that one tear was gone, I almost felt giddy. It was over. No long distance relationship. It would have never have worked out anyway.

I shook out my arms, as if to shake off any excess stress, before heading back to my house. Mom wasn't home yet, so I started dinner. Despite the bulkiness of my cast, I stirred up a veggie soup.

I heard the door open downstairs and decided I would tell Mom about the break-up over dinner. I dished out two bowls of soup, after Mom entered the kitchen. It must have started to rain, because she was sopping wet. I looked out the window, and sure enough it was raining.

Am I that unobservant, I wondered? If I would have taken a moment to listen, I would have heard rain beating against the windowpane. I set both bowls of soup on the table and poured us both an orange juice.

"Mom, I have to talk to you about something," I said, biting my lip and running my hand through my hair.

"Mm?" Mom asked, sitting down and digging into her soup. She almost spit it back into the bowl, it was so hot.

"It's hot," I warned.

"Little late," she pointed out.

I sat down across from her and stirred my soup, slowly. *It is like a Band-Aid. Pull it off quickly and get it over with,* I reminded myself.

"I broke up with Harrison," I said.

She almost dropped her spoon.

"You did?!" she exclaimed.

"Well, we kind of broke up with each other." I explained everything from after the boy at the library to before the single tear.

"Are you ok? You know, I thought things were good between you two," she said.

"I just don't think a long distance relationship would be healthy. It would be really hard," I explained.

Plus, Harrison and I had been together for over year now, and any feelings we had for one another were weakening with time. It was time to move on. There were always more fish in the sea, as my grandmother used to say. I wanted to find one that swam with me, not one that naturally drifted away. Then Mom quoted that very phrase of my grandma's.

"There are always more fish in the sea," Mom said.

Olympic Bound

It was sort of a family tradition to utter that phrase, whenever someone in the family was just out of a relationship.

I laughed in my head at the thought. Grandma said it to Mom; Great-grandma said it to Grandma, and so on.

***

The next day, I called Emily, Jasmine, and Kate, all in turn, and told them the news. Kate insisted that I go with her and Jasmine the next day to the beach.

"If you let me bring, Emily," I said.

"No way! Okay. Do you want to know why Jasmine and I don't like her so much?" Kate asked.

"Yeah!" I said, instantly.

Ever since I had found out that they didn't like her, I wondered what the reason was.

"Don't tell Jasmine I told you, ok, or anyone. Not even your Mom?" she demanded, nervously.

"O-o-o-okay," I said.

"Promise," she urged.

"Promise," I said back, dying to know what on earth turned two of my best friends against Emily. She was just so sweet! It didn't make sense!

Before, I had thought it might be over something silly. But now, it seemed like this might be something serious.

"Emily killed Jasmine's father," Kate finally blurted.

Chapter 25 - Unbelievable

"What?!" I screamed into the phone.

That couldn't be true. Emily was a perky, adaptable, sweet girl that cried when she saw a dead bug. Plus, she would be in prison if she had killed someone, wouldn't she? I heard Kate take a deep breath.

"Emily and Jasmine and I use to be close friends, even before we knew Taffeta," she began. "Emily was over at Jasmine's house when it happened. We went up into Jasmine's old tree house, which is gone now, and I discovered a broken board and yelled down to Jasmine's dad, Pete, to tell him about it. He came up to check it out and joked about something. I can't remember what it was, but Emily pushed him! I don't think she meant to hurt him, but she pushed him, and he lost his balance . . ." Kate paused and took another deep, shuddering breath. "He fell back over the railing—it only came up to his waist—and he fell all the way to the ground and landed . . . on his head." I covered my mouth with my hand.

"But Emily didn't mean to do it," I protested. It wasn't fair that they could be so mean to her for something she didn't mean to do.

But then I thought of my dad. If Emily had killed him, even by accident, I probably wouldn't have been able to look her in the face again, ever.

"But she still killed him, and . . . if only you had seen him," Kate said. "He was in a weird position with his neck twisted too far, and there was blood everywhere."

My stomach lurched with the urge to vomit.

"There was this big lawsuit, but Emily was not held responsible, since it was an accident. She was only ten at the time," Kate continued.

Suddenly, I wished this conversation was over.

"Thank you for telling me that, Kate," I said, "but my mom is coming. I've got to go."

"Bye, Taylor," she said. I hung up and sat down on my bed, heaving.

Sad memories of Dad and Mel broke to the surface. I had been so good at burying my emotions deep within, that the sudden pain was like a shock wave rippling around my body, closing me in a trap.

I felt sick, but I didn't feel like I had to cry. I just wanted to puke. I raced to the bathroom and filled the toilet with left-over veggie stew.

After puking I felt better—sort of. I definitely felt less nauseated, but just as depressed as before. I took deep breaths and tried to push Mel and Dad away from my mind. But trying not to think of something only made me think about it twice as much.

I tried a different tactic. Watching a movie was one way to zone out. I asked Mom if she wanted to watch something.

"Sure, Honey," she said, plopping down on the couch next to me. "Anything on?" she asked.

I shrugged and flipped on the TV.

By the looks of it, the most compelling thing on at the moment was *America's Funniest Home Videos*, but it made Mom angry because she thought most of the videos were set-ups.

"Go ahead," she sighed, as I realized I was hovering over the channel that occupied *America's Funniest Home Videos*.

I watched, as a guy ran a motorcycle into a plastic, above-ground pool and broke through it, spilling out all the water along with his bike.

After a few minutes of watching, I didn't feel any better. My theory, that the TV would get my mind off the topic of Dad and Mel, was proved wrong quite swiftly.

I sighed, sadly, at my discovery. Mom looked at me from the corner of her eye, realizing something was wrong.

"You, ok, Sweetheart?" she asked, worriedly.

"Yeah, fine," I replied.

I turned my attention back to the TV just in time to see a dog bark, "I Love You" and a group of people that were skating, fall though the ice.

***

The next day, Harrison called me. I picked up the phone on the second ring and held it up to my ear, wondering why he was calling.

"Hey, it's me," he said, quietly.

"Hey, Harrison," I said, almost in the same timid voice as him.

"I just wanted to see how you were doing," he said.

"Good," I said. "You?"

"Good," he said.

"Taylor, the reason I'm calling is that I was wondering if you still want me to go to Trials with you. If not, then I won't go. It might get awkward," he said.

"Harrison, you're welcome to come," I assured him. "But you don't have to."

"But do you want me there?" he asked.

I thought for a while before coming up with an honest answer.

"Yes, if you'll come as a friend," I said.

"Alright, I'll come with you then," he said. I could hear his smile through the phone.

He was hurting, and I still didn't get it. He broke up with *me*.

"Great, bye," I said.

"Bye, Taylor," he said and hung up.

***

I managed not to think too much of Dad or Mel while I shopped with Emily. She was getting dangerously low on clothes that fit and weren't holey. I had felt bad for Emily this past year. Her dad got laid off work, so not only were her shopping days limited, but she had to postpone going to college. She was hoping they could have enough money for her to go by next year, especially now that she was eligible for more financial assistance.

But my new knowledge of the thing about Jasmine's dad bothered me all the while, until I finally couldn't stand not to say something.

"Emily, why didn't you tell me about Jasmine's dad?" I asked. I waited to see how she would respond.

"What about him? Didn't he die or something?" she said, casually.

"Kate told me," I informed her.

"Told you what?" she asked, getting annoyed.

"Don't worry, Emily, I won't tell anyone. I promised. I just want to hear your side of the story," I said, calmly.

"My side of the story of what?!" Emily looked at me, exasperated now.

"I just want to know what really happened, because Kate can be known for embellishing," I continued.

"Taylor, I don't have the faintest idea of what you're talking about!" she said, curtly.

Now I was starting to get a little mad. Couldn't she confide in me? We were best friends, after all.

"Fine, I will spell it out for you. How you killed her dad!" I exclaimed.

Olympic Bound

She stared back at me, stunned.

"Kate told you that I killed Jasmine's father?" she asked, sadly, suddenly sounding small and mousy again.

"So, it isn't true?" I asked.

"No, and I am hurt that you think I am capable of murder," she said, harshly.

"They said you did it by accident, knocking him out of a treehouse," I explained.

I was fuming mad at Kate for telling me such an awful story. How could she? Especially since she had to know it would remind me of my own loss of my dad and Mel. Even if reminding me of my own horrors was unintentional, surely Kate knew that I would ask Emily about it, which is now putting me through this awkward situation.

"Emily, I'm so sorry," I apologized.

Emily didn't reply. Instead she hung a top, she was examining, back on the rack.

"I think I want to go home," she said.

I nodded and followed her to my car to take her home.

I was definitely going to have a long talk with Kate.

***

After I had dropped Emily off, I went to my house and pulled out my phone. Kate didn't take long to pick up.

"Hey, Taylor," she said, nonchalantly.

"Why did you lie about Emily?" I demanded.

"I didn't," she replied. "I told you not to tell anyone; that includes her. She doesn't remember doing it. It like erased part of her memory she was so mortified. She was shocked. She forgot everything."

I wondered if she was telling the truth. But judging by her voice, she believed every word she was saying.

"Oh," I say, finally. Not quite knowing who to believe, I apologized and hung up the phone.

Was it really possible to just forget something like that, or rather have a bad memory wiped clean from your brain?

I pondered the thought for a while. It seemed crazy, but I guessed it fit. I needed a distraction from this mess. As weird as it sounded, I wished that I could go and jump in the pool and swim, but I knew I couldn't. My wrist wouldn't allow it, yet. So instead, I dressed to go to the gym to let off steam with another workout.

Then, something caught my eye. It was a book on the shelf—a book Dad had loved to read. I pulled it off the shelf.

Olympic Bound

When I opened it, something slipped out —a letter Dad had sent me when I was staying with my aunt down here in Florida for a past spring break. This time I couldn't hold back the tears.

I read through the letter several times, loving to see his handwriting. He wrote it on an Indiana postcard with the picture of the woods on it.

It didn't look like a photo taken in Indiana, though. Everything looked overly green, like the picture had been painted on to look more appealing. I wondered where he had bought it.

I read the letter for a final time, and decided that I shouldn't torture myself any longer.

Dear Taylor,

How is Florida? You tan yet? I took Mel to the new laser-tag place and I promise to take you when you get home. We have been having a bit of bad luck, though. The blue Ford car broke down. A branch fell through the roof in that big storm we had and I didn't get that promotion. Oh, well! Onwards and upwards! Remember to keep swimming! Mom, Mel, and I are all missing you.

Love,

KD Lee Writes

Dad

Determined more than ever, to stay strong while I healed from my wrist injury, I walked out the door to do my workout.

Olympic Bound

CHAPTER 26 - SURPRISE

Mom came home early one day. She walked through the door and was simply beaming.

"I just told your coach about your broken wrist, and he said he knows a chiropractor that may be able to help you!" she said. "I called this chiropractor, and she said to bring you over at the end of her day, today. So, get dressed, and let's go!"

"A chiropractor?" I asked. "But what can a chiropractor do for a broken wrist?"

"She said that she can get you a waterproof-cast cover for swimming!" Mom said. "And she can explain how you can keep in shape while you heal! She said you have plenty of time to be ready for Qualifications, if you are willing to do the rehab!"

"Really! Awesome," I said. "But how much would that cost?"

"She said she would only charge us if you make it, and you can pay her by endorsing chiropractic when you are famous," Mom said.

"Seriously?" I asked.

"Yes! So, let's go! What do we have to lose?" Mom asked.

***

We pulled up to a small house that was converted to an office. I didn't understand what the chiropractor did, but I felt amazing when she was done with my treatment. Even my wrist felt better.

She gave me supplements to support the healing of my bones. She also gave me dietary advice to help me build and maintain muscle. Then, she gave me a pamphlet of exercises and stretches to help me keep my swimming muscles strong while my wrist was impaired. She also ordered a waterproof cast that would fit me perfectly.

She explained that we could remove the cast once my bones had healed enough to handle a removable cast. She explained that it was important to get the wrist moving as soon as possible, or else I would heal with a wrist that didn't move properly. It was important to keep the mobility in my wrist, or it would mess with my swimming, which I couldn't afford.

Olympic Bound

She even arranged for several personal trainers to volunteer their time to work with me! She spent all of this time with me after her normal business hours! She was so nice. It seemed odd to me that she wasn't even charging Mom for her work. I was glad there were such good people in this world.

"I hope to pay you back for this one day," I said to her, before we left her office.

"I believe you will," she said, with a kind smile.

KD Lee Writes

Olympic Bound

Summer

(Again)

KD Lee Writes

Olympic Bound

CHAPTER 27 – TWO SECONDS

Finally! It was time for my appointment to see if I could try swimming without any type of splint on my wrist. We were in the car and on the way to the chiropractor's office. Just in time, too. Trials were just around the corner! I had missed over a month of valuable, intense swimming practice time, and no doubt my wrist still would be sore during my practice before Trials.

I was giddy as the chiropractor took off my splint and examined my wrist. I was good to go, yet my wrist was stiff and tender, and my forearm was still a little weak.

"Just don't overdo it in the pool, alright?" the chiropractor told me. "Your wrist still isn't one-hundred percent. If it gets sore, put the swimming caste back on."

Despite the chiropractor's warning, I planned on getting in the pool to test how far I could swim, free of the splint, as soon as I got home.

Mom drove me, so I pushed her to hurry home. I had to get into the pool. After an hour of therapeutic swimming in the little pool, I planned on meeting up with Emily at the YMCA.

My wrist bothered me slightly, as I swam, but it was not, as bad as I had expected. I didn't know if I was swimming slower, but I sure felt like I was. I hoped my time would improve without having to swim with a waterproof splint.

My swim was cut short because it rained, so I called Emily to ask if she could meet me early. She happily agreed.

I was glad to see she carried with her a timer, an object I had forgotten to bring in my rush. I really wanted to see if I was actually slower. I had gotten a lot better since Qualifications, and I hoped that it all hadn't been lost due to a stupid handstand.

"Hey Taylor!" she said, brightly, obviously having forgiven me already.

"Hey, Emily," I said. "Thanks for meeting me early. I wasn't sure you would after our last conversation."

"Oh, yes," Emily said. "I called Kate to confront her, and she didn't pick up. So I called her home number, and her mom answered. I told her what she said about me, and she ended up apologizing. Did you know Kate is seeing a therapist and is on anti-depressant medication, because she has compulsive lying disorder?"

"Oh, my gosh! Seriously? That explains so much!" I exclaimed.

"I know," Emily continued. "That is why Jasmine didn't like me. Kate was telling terrible stories about me. But at least she told you such a crazy story, that you had reason to doubt her."

"No joke! Wow," I exclaimed.

Happy that mystery was solved, and not wanting to dwell on it, I looked longingly at the pool. The water was beckoning me.

"Hey, do you mind timing me for one lap, so I can see if I've lost some of my speed?" I asked, eyeing the timer.

"Not at all," she said, happy to change the topic as well.

I dove into the water and began swimming freestyle all the way to the end. I was two seconds slower than last time. That may not seem like much, but seconds were lifetimes whenever you were racing. It was the same with running and car races.

I groaned at the news. And now, it seemed I had tweaked my wrist too. I would have to work on my technique this week and try to get my speed back. I was a whole two seconds slower on just on one lap? Unbelievable!

I timed Emily, next. She was pleased to beat her best time.

"Nice swim," I commented, giving her a high-five with my left hand, remembering to be overly cautious with my right wrist.

She insisted that we go out to eat and celebrate. So after three hours of swimming, we headed off to get some food. We went to Five Guys, which in my opinion had the best burgers in Florida. Their fries were amazing, too. They were cooked in peanut oil. One final reason I liked Five Guys was that it had free peanuts.

We ordered, and while we waited for our number to be called, I, again, congratulated Emily on setting her personal record, earlier.

"Thanks," Emily replied, before popping a peanut into her mouth.

My mouth watered waiting for my cheeseburger with lettuce, tomato, and onion. I heard them call our number, 57, so I went up to claim our food.

"57?" the lady questioned.

I nodded, and she smiled as she handed me the bag. I pulled out our hamburgers and the cup of fries. There was still a pile of fries in the bottom of the bag, after we finished the ones in the cup. Unwrapping the foil surrounding the burger, I took my first, juicy bite. Yum! Just as good as I remembered. I didn't get to go there, often.

"What do you think of Charles?" Emily asked me, suddenly.

I scanned my brain. Did I know a Charles?

"Um, who is that?" I asked.

"A guy from school; he kind of asked me on a date," she said.

"Oh, what year is he?" I asked.

"Senior," Emily said, dreamily.

"Maybe if you gave me a little description, I would remember him?" I suggested.

"He has black hair, brown eyes, some freckles. He is short, maybe two inches shorter than me," Emily said. But she was so tall that two inches shorter than her would be considered normal.

I thought I knew who she was talking about, but I wasn't sure. The guy I was thinking of just kind of hung back and didn't talk much.

"Is he shy?" I asked.

"Yeah, pretty shy," she replied.

"I think I know who you are talking about," I answered, still not positive.

"I wish I could go cheer you on at Trials, but my parents wouldn't hear of it. We just can't afford it," she said, sadly.

"I wish you could come, too, but I understand and that is fine," I said.

"You'll have to have your mom video it or something," she said, excitedly. "Or, maybe, I'll see you on the news," she added, hopefully.

"That would be cool," I replied.

"How is your wrist?" she asked.

"Not broken," I said, trying to sound upbeat.

"That's good . . . I guess," she said.

"So tell me more about Charles," I said, changing the subject.

Emily brightened with the new subject.

"Well, he is taking me to the movies Friday night. We are seeing the new James Fiffer movie," she said.

"I thought you hate James Fiffer," I said, confused.

"But Charles doesn't," she said, staring off into space.

Olympic Bound

"I hope you guys have fun," I said, finding a break in the conversation to take a bite of my food.

"We will," she replied, as she plopped a single ketchup-covered fry into her mouth.

I wrinkled my nose in disgust. I hated ketchup. It was filled with more corn syrup than tomatoes.

"Are you nervous for Trials?" Emily asked.

"Very," I admitted.

"I would be shaking with nerves diving into the water," Emily assured me.

"This will be even more nerve-wracking than qualifiers," I said.

Not only was there going to be a large crowd this time, but if I lost, I would have to live with how close I had come.

"Just win, ok?" she said.

"I'll try," I promised.

"I really hope you do well," Emily said.

KD Lee Writes

Olympic Bound

CHAPTER 28 – PAY OFF

"I'm so nervous," I said. I was literally shaking. There was a whole stadium of spectators watching me swim this time, and the place was swarming with news reporters determined to trap one of the poor swimmers for an interview.

I was in a "ready room" like before. I clutched my swim cap in one hand and my goggles in the other.

"You'll be great," Mom assured me.

I was so nervous that my lack of practice, caused by my accident, would cost me a chance to be in the Olympics. Why had I been stupid enough to risk hurting myself before Trials? I was still beating myself up over it.

I took deep breaths and did light stretches to limber up while I waited. Mom hovered around me. Harrison was already seated in the stadium next to Mom's empty seat.

A group of girls were swimming right before me. When then finished, I would be up. I clutched my stomach, suddenly, feeling sick. This one event could determine my whole future.

***

When it was time, I walked up to the starting block and got in position, eyeing the many people everywhere. I tried to zone them out and only focus on swimming the 50-meter freestyle.

The gun fired and I dove in. The water closed in around me. I broke into my freestyle stroke and kicked my feet as fast as I could, making the windmill with my arms again. My legs felt stronger than ever before.

Then I was there, before I knew it, on the other side of the pool. Had I won? Had I passed? I looked over. Only one girl had made it before me. I had come in second!

In that moment, all of the workouts with the personal trainers, the extra stretching and workouts at home, and the awkwardness of swimming with a waterproof cast and splint, and finally swimming daily without any cast had really paid off!

After

KD Lee Writes

Chapter 29 – The Interview

The man slipped a medal over my head. I had just won the Olympics for the first time! My heart was pumping, as I smiled to the crowd around me. The reporters arrived in waves, and I agreed to an interview with one of them.

"How does it feel to be holding the gold for your first time?" she asked.

"Awesome," I said. "I just feel very fortunate that I got this opportunity to compete in the Olympics." A short, but sweet, answer.

Not forgetting my promise, I quickly added, "I would not be here if it wasn't for my chiropractor."

"Why do you say that?" the reporter asked.

"I broke my wrist less than four months before the Trials," I said. "Usually that is the end for an Olympic hopeful. She was able to get me, not only better, but better in time to make it through the Trials."

"Interesting," the reporter said. "How many years did you train before you made it to the Olympics?"

I decided not to mention the different periods of downtime and instead answered, "Ever since I was four. My dad was my biggest inspiration."

"Is he here, today?" the reporter asked.

"I wish he was, he died a few years back," I replied.

"I'm sorry," he said. "Is your mom here?"

"Yes, she is." I looked past the reporter to my mom. The camera man swiveled the camera around to get a shot of her.

"Ms. Reeve, how do you feel about everything your daughter has accomplished?" The reporter asked her and held up a microphone to her.

Mom's face was flushed red. She hated to be in the spotlight.

"I am very proud of her," she said.

"Do you come to all her swimming events?" the reporter asked.

"I've never missed one," she said. The camera turned back to me.

Olympic Bound

"Tell us something about yourself that our viewers would like to know," the reporter instructed.

I wondered what he wanted me to say. Where I am from? My favorite foods? I didn't want to say anything lame like that. I wanted to tell them something important. Then it came to me. It was so obvious.

"My father died swimming in the ocean—he drowned," I said. "But I know he would still want me to keep fighting for my dream, so I worked hard, practicing every day until I could achieve my dream, not just for me, but for the memories of the loved ones I have lost. The impossible has been achieved before, so anything is possible if you put your mind to it."

Epilogue

The twelve year-old, Lucy did very well in Trials, but she didn't get first or second to make it to the Olympics. The reporters were swarming around her due to her age, despite her not winning. She is going to try again in three years.

Penny made it to the Olympics with me, as well as Joy, but Ava didn't.

I made it with 50 free, 100 free, 200 medley, 400 medley, and 50 breaststroke. I surprised myself with the score. It is crazy what a little bit of adrenaline will do for you.

Harrison continued going to the local college but we grew apart, regardless. Emily and Jasmine became friends after learning of Kate and her condition. Kate went off to a rehab center. Emily, ended up going to a college the same year as I did. I grew apart from all of them because of college and life in general.

I never got over Dad or Mel. They would always have a place in my heart no matter what happened or how many years went by. I still think about them every day, and likely will until the day I die.

KD Lee Writes

Olympic Bound

COMING SOON

Getaway Plan

(A Mystery for 14 & up)

The Morgan Series

Book III

Morgan's Baby Sister

(A Realistic Fiction for Ages 8-12)

KD Lee Writes

Interview with Author

Q: What inspired you to write about a girl that wants to go to the Olympics?

A: I love to swim. I never thought about trying to get into the Olympics, but I thought a story about a girl fighting to make her dream come true would be a good one.

Q: How long did it take you to write this novel?

A: Three months in total, but it's the editing that takes forever!

Q: What do you like to write about most: mysteries, Sci-Fi, fantasy, realistic fiction, or nonfiction?

A: I don't favor a category. I like to write about anything. I must admit though, nonfiction isn't as fun as fiction because then you can't use your imagination as much. You are forced to stick to the facts.

Q: What is the first novel you ever wrote and how old were you when you wrote it?

A: The first novel I ever wrote was called Morgan's Summer, and I finished it when I was ten years old. I published it the following year.

Q: Do you plan on being an author your whole life or switching your career path when you are older?

A: I would like to be an author my whole life, but that doesn't mean that I can't have other jobs as well. Being an author means my job schedule is flexible when I don't have readings or book signings.

Q: What is your favorite part about being an author?

A: There are many reasons I like being an author, but the one I like most is that I can have a career doing what I love instead of it just being a hobby.

Q: What is the greatest inspiration for your novels?

A: My brother and everyday life. I draw from my experiences a lot, but everything that happens in my books are made up or embellished.

ABOUT THE AUTHOR

KD, pronounced "Kay-Dee," was born in 2003. She lives in the country near Bloomington, IN. She is homeschooled by her grandmother, DD, who is a retired school teacher. She has a younger brother. She enjoys swimming, playing her guitar, wakeboarding, golf, and other activities. Writing, however, is her true passion. KD wrote her first book, *Bad Lilly*, when she was four. Her first article was published in a youth magazine when she was eight. Shortly afterwards, KD started writing her *Morgan's* series. She finished the first book, *Morgan's Summer*, before her eleventh birthday. KD is currently working on many other novels.

ABOUT THE BOOK

Taylor loves the water and swimming. With her father's encouragement, she starts training for the summer Olympics with the dream of going for gold! Then, a tragedy occurs, involving a horrible loss, a large move, and such a change in lifestyle that causes Taylor to spiral into a deep depression. Can she still fight for her dream and become an Olympic swimmer? Or, will her unbelievably bad luck get in the way?

KD Lee Writes